Pierre Motteux

Safe Sex is essential: your very life may depend on it. Please remember that some of the sexual practices that are featured in this work of fiction (written in an era that pre-dates lethal STDs) are dangerous and they are not recommended or in any way endorsed by the publishers; by the same token, we do not condone any form of non-consensual sex for any reason: it is reprehensible and illegal and should never become a part of a person's real life: rather it should remain firmly in the realm of sexual fantasy.

Havana Harlot
Past Venus Press
London 2007

Past Venus Press
is an imprint of
THE *Erotic* Print Society
EPS, 1st Floor, 17 Harwood Road,
LONDON SW6 4QP

Tel: +44 (0) 207 736 5800
Email: eros@eroticprints.org
Web: www.eroticprints.org

© 2007 MacHo Ltd, London UK

ISBN : 978-1-904989-32 -5

Printed and bound in Spain by S.A de Litografia. Barcelona

HAVANA HARLOT

Pierre Motteux

*E*PS

PRELUDE

On his thirtieth birthday, Lieutenant Charles Longworthy of the 1st U.S. Volunteer Cavalry Regiment, also known as Teddy Roosevelt's 'Roughriders' hid his army-issue, single-action, Colt 45 'Peacemaker' behind a Havana prostitute's water closet. The war was over bar the shouting. He had become outrageously drunk celebrating with some of his fellow officers and there had been a gunfight in the seedy *taberna* downstairs. Nothing fatal, but some lowlife had been wounded and was screaming like a stuck pig, emitting a stream of loud, high-pitched Spanish invective. The local *policía* were called and the situation was becoming more embarrassing by the moment. This was 'conduct unbecoming' and he and his brother officers knew it. Most of them were married and it would cause a fearful scandal if they were caught in what amounted to a brothel masquerading as a bar. The group of drunken officers dispersed and Charlie made his way back with the prostitute to her room above, where earlier he had enjoyed her considerable charms. Delighted by the prospect of another payment from her virile *yanqui*, she was only too pleased to supply an alibi of sorts. This included undoing his fly-buttons as he lay sprawled on her bed and taking his limp, exhausted penis in her mouth until its owner was able to provide her with a tolerable erection. But this time his gun failed to discharge.

Charlie's real gun was another matter. The *policía* were swarming over the ramshackle building now. It had to be hidden and she showed him just where. It would be safe with Teresa. Little *Teté* would look after it for him... for a few more dollars.

He could come back any time and claim it, she said.

He never did. The loss of a piece of army ordnance earned him a severe reprimand and cancellation of any leave; there was even talk of a court marshal. When the regiment disbanded, Charlie was able to joke about the whole incident with his fellow Ivy Leaguers over a game of polo. But it was an experience he would not easily forget.

Chapter 1

The flies were the worst of the many indignities. Even the odours of decayed fish from the nearby wharves, and the sharp, acrid smell of male urine from the gutter outside her window had become part of the accepted background. She was aware that her own body had begun to add to the aroma. Next to the flies, she hated more than all the rest to feel the acute needs of her unwashed body.

She attempted to shift her position, but the bonds that kept her spread-eagled on the soiled bed linen were not loose enough to permit much movement. She looked down through the valley of her proud young breasts, over the creamy flat tummy and the blonde curls of her womanly forest, to the iron rails at the foot of the bed. The ropes that secured her ankles were tied to the two corner posts.

The shifting movement had caused a little chafing, but her ankles didn't bother her as much as her wrists. She couldn't see them but she could imagine the red rawness of the skin from the burning sensations. Yet, this misery paled by comparison with the flies.

The insects, which had awakened her by crawling over the damp stickiness of her exposed vulva had flown away as she moved. She knew she would have to move repeatedly to keep them away. She tried to scream past the gag in her mouth, but the only sound it inside was in her own head, where the pressure was so great, that she gave up.

If only the Boston jeunesse dorée could see her now! Helen Longworthy, princess of the tennis court, pacesetter of the flashy younger set, untouchable virgin with a reputation for semi-frigidity! If she had only given herself to Harry, or Bill! She choked back a sob, knowing from bitter experience how much more miserable she'd be if she let herself start crying with that gag in her mouth.

Some flies had returned to feast in the forest of her sticky golden curls. She rolled her hips, and the movement made all but one stubborn insect buzz off. She could feel it moving across the moist outer lips, then into the slit of her sensitive inner lips. She thrust her hip upward, and it flew out and away, joining one of the groups of its fellows hovering in the air, or crawling on the many unclean surfaces in the shabby room.

The perspiration was gathering on her skin, and it added to the discomfort and to the closeness of the room, as if the June warmth and the humidity of the harbour area weren't enough.

She tried to take her thoughts off her misery, to get away from the unendurable present. Not daring to think of what might lie in the immediate future, she could only dwell on the past. And the most immediate experiences of the last two days were so luridly etched in her memory that they flashed past her all too slowly.

* * *

The sights and sounds of Havana were novel and intriguing to Helen Longworthy. Her four years of Spanish were just enough to add spice to the adventure. She and her mother did all the translating and interpreting for the family. Papa Longworthy's meagre vocabulary, acquired during the the Spanish American war of 1898, was almost completely lost, and Frank had chosen French for his language courses. Well, little brother was anxious to do the honours when they got to Haiti. He insisted that he didn't care much for the Cubans.

At seventeen, Helen was in full flower. Her luscious body and charming personality were almost the exact replica of her mother at the same age. But her goals were different. Ruth Longworthy had become a bride at her daughter's age, marrying Charles Hiram Longworthy II in 1892, and they had settled in Boston, where the family business was based. Lieutenant Longworthy and his bride were a handsome couple, and though not quite a 'Boston Brahmin' family, they certainly moved in those circles. Helen enjoyed looking at the old photographs of their wedding and early married life in the numerous albums at home.

Unlike her mother, Helen wanted a few more years of freedom before committing her entire life and responsibilities to another. She had her hands full with the young males of her acquaintance, finding it difficult to convince them of her true wishes for (at least temporary) independence.

But underneath, the juices of her flowering womanhood ran swift and warm. She knew her susceptibility to the healthy maleness of her friends, and took great care to avoid temptations. She blushed when she thought of how she had been aroused even by her own father, on several occasions. Well, she only had herself to blame herself for that. The constant denial of her womanly urges increased her sensitivities. It was no wonder that being embraced by a proud and loving father could stir her more unmentionable desires.

Especially a virile man like Papa

Longworthy. Even now, at 42, he was more man than many of his juniors. Helen had seen numerous females make a play for the handsome landowner. His six-foot-one frame was in trim condition, only ten pounds heavier than he'd been in those wedding photos. And he still satisfied the constant hungers of his loyal and lusty wife, whose daughter was all too well acquainted with her mother's passionate and earthy nature.

Helen still recalled clearly the scene she had witnessed by accident only a week before the trip started. One night she had been unable to sleep, and decided to take a nocturnal stroll. The warm evening and the high-walled security of the Longworthy mansion had lulled her normal precautions, and she simply tossed a diaphanous robe on her naked body, and walked slowly down the little avenue of trees to the large ornamental pool and elaborate baroque fountain at the bottom of the walled garden. Bare footing over the cool marble, she had stopped short at the sight of her parents on the little veranda of the summer house at the far side of the big pool. Her mother's ripe body lay in serene repose on a carelessly flung quilt, elegant in the creamy skin that glowed pale under bright moonlight. Helen had darted out of sight in the darkness of some nearby shrubbery.

From her shadowy vantage point, Helen watched as her equally naked father knelt at his wife's feet. His short, brown hair glinted in the moonlight, and Helen could see bright droplets of water on his muscular body. Obviously, her parents had decided on a midnight swim, believing her to be in bed. Frank wasn't due home from college until the weekend.

Papa Longworthy's hands took the slim ankles and moved them aside and upward. He went forward, and his face pushed into the valley of Ruth's lovely breasts. Helen's breath caught as she watched the kisses he bestowed on the creamy mounds. Her own full globes ached as she watched him nibbling and tonguing the peaks, and she felt her nipples distend in sympathetic passion.

A piercing feeling of guilt urged her to move her away from the scene. It was a private thing, between a man and a woman. What's more, it was her parents, her father and mother. But her hungry body was tingling with its own fevers, and in the self-imposed restrictions of her young life, this was the only direct sexual play she had ever encountered. It was too much for her curiosity. She moved quietly and stealthily along the shadowed edges of the tall shrubs that surrounded the end of the pool. She didn't stop until she was behind the bush nearest the naked couple.

She was only a few yards from the damp bodies, and she could hear her mother's low, purring sounds, and the wet, lapping sounds of her father's tongue and lips. He had moved down, now, across the sleek belly into the blonde, feathery curls below.

Wide-eyed, Helen knelt in the grass, her hands clutching her fevered breasts, fingering the swollen nipples frantically. She saw the creamy thighs open wide, and one of the feet, with its neatly pedicured nails pointed right at Helen's hiding place.

Charlie Longworthy's lips and tongue were searching tenderly among the blonde curls, and Helen knew he had found what he sought when Ruth's purring sounds became a louder, continuous moan, and the full hips rose from the quilt. Ruth's hands reached down and grasped the brown curls of her lover's head, pulling the ministering mouth tighter to her damp, heated flesh.

He's kissing her… quim! Helen thought to herself. My God! That must feel so wonderful! The girl dropped one hand from its clutching, squeezing movements at her breast. It sought the blonde jungle at the juncture of her own quivering thighs. Her fingers parted the wet lips, and began to massage the stiff little bud of her passion.

Ohh! I wish it were me! To have those lips and that tongue in my sex would drive me wild! Helen's hand was covered now with the hot liquid of her passion's lubricant. Her breath was laboured, and a jellylike weakness was creeping through her thighs and loins.

"Charlie! Oh, my darling, drink me! Drink me dry!" Ruth's trembling voice on Helen's ears excited her even more. She saw the wiggling hips moving in spasms as the climax built. Then a shuddering jerk of the moonlit body gave Helen the knowledge that her mother had found a glorious release. At that moment, her own orgasm began, and she shook under the intensity of its effect on her body.

Helen took her weight off one knee, and moved her thighs close together. It squeezed her hand in place, nestling it tight in the sloppy, swollen lips, and maintaining a glowing feeling with its pressure on her most sensitive spot.

Charlie had changed his position, and Helen could see the rigid tool of his loving art. The three-quarter view afforded her all too clearly a complete awareness of what took place.

Ruth's thighs were drawn back and even farther apart, now. The gleaming pink meat of her womanhood was vulnerably spread wide, and Helen could see the juices flowing down it. Then Charlie's body hid the pulsing love-mouth as he positioned himself over his wife.

Helen moved quietly to place herself in another position, not able to force herself to leave, knowing that she had to see everything. Then she watched as the purplish pink head of the rigid lance lay lightly in the wet lips Ruth's raised hips, and Charlie's hips went forward. The shaft buried itself in the depths, and the sight of its hairy luggage swinging against the wet portals below it was too much for Helen.

Again, she worked feverishly in the sloppy heat of her crotch. Now, the anxious massage seemed not enough. As she watched the slow strokes of the plunging rod, she thrust a finger of her other hand into the tightness of her own virginal passage. The sharp sensation of near-pain almost made her cry out, but she retained enough awareness in the midst of her extreme passion to bite back the sound.

She gave up the attempt, afraid of betraying her presence, and contented herself with massaging her hard bud and rolling her nipples-first one, then the other-between the fingers of her other hand.

Oh-h! If just watching can do this to me, what would it be like to have a wonderful prick like that inside me? It looks so good, I could almost crawl over there and put it in my mouth! My God! What kind of a nymphomaniac am I, anyhow? Her breath was sobbing in her throat as she worked her fingers in the slippery swollen meat of her nether lips.

Then she watched her father cease his plunging, grab her mother's buttocks, and press hard against her. Ruth's husky voice was pleading.

"Fuck me deep, Charlie! Ohhhhhh! Now! Squirt the spunk into me! My cunt's so hungry for you!" The coarse words from the normally refined and quiet woman seemed to excite her husband tremendously. He cried out softly, and his buttocks squeezed together.

The vulgar words had a strong effect on Helen, too. It was all she could do to keep from crying out herself, as she watched his muscles spasm, knowing that he was pumping some delightfully exciting elixir into the hot, female depths. She smothered her sounds as she moaned softly to herself, feeling the huge wave of heat tear through her body. A warm extra flow of juice poured over her hand, and she fell over backward and lay, trembling in the cool grass.

It was lucky that Charlie and Ruth took their time about getting up off the quilt. Helen's legs were like water as she tried to get to her feet, and they barely supported her as she slipped through the shadows back to the house. By the time she reached the French windows of her room, and entered, little streams of fluid were running down both thighs, tickling the sensitive skin.

She rushed into her shower and bathed quickly, ending up with a cold needle-spray. It seemed to help calm her down.

But, lying in bed, afterward, she kept seeing the actions she had witnessed, and before she realized it was happening, her hand was again seeking the heated and swollen lips. When she found how slippery and wet they had become from those recalled sights, she gave up all hope of restraint, and worked herself through another fevered climax, until she lay spent, panting for breath. Then she had to shower all over again.

* * *

Recalling the shameful episode had affected her strongly, Helen knew. She could feel the flow of her juices running down the crevice of her crotch, and wetting her tense anus before it added to the stains on the soiled linen. She twitched her hips and moved upward to shake off the flies, again, and to try to relieve the hot, tingling feeling around her genitals.

She fought back the sobs again, as she remembered how she had spied on her parents that night. They were wonderful parents. The mother who was so like her daughter in appearance, and apparently in passion, and the handsome, virile, accomplished father, who was so proud of his girls. She remembered how pleased he was the other morning – was it really only two days ago?

* * *

They had left the hotel and started to see the sights of Havana. They intended to spend only two days there, until Charlie could make contact with a Cuban competitor whose firm he considered buying to merge with his own American company.

Helen and Ruth were dressed exactly alike, in matching blouses and long skirts, even to the charming little boots. Charlie walked between them, and his pride in their beauty was evident to all who looked, including the girls themselves.

Tired as they were when they returned to the hotel, they were laughing and full of enjoyment from the novelty of the visit. Frank had awakened from a nap in his room, and had joined them for a few minutes before going off on his own to look up a friend who had been an exchange student at his school.

Then Charlie and Ruth collapsed in their room, and Helen rested for a short while. But she became restless, and decided to take a walk in the verdant little park she could see from her window. She left a note on her table, and headed for the cool shade of the tropical greenery.

Looking back, she cursed herself for the hundredth time for her foolhardiness.

Walking through the park, which turned out to be quite small, shabby, and very dusty, once was she inside it, she had seen a curious little boutique across the boulevard, and had walked over to window shop.

Later, when she realized that she had walked several blocks down the street, and was entering a rather disreputable-looking neighbourhood, she turned and crossed the boulevard and started back to the hotel.

When the carriage first pulled up beside her, she thought it was merely a cab touting for business, and looked up at the coachman, telling him that she didn't need a ride, but thank you very much all the same. She wanted to show him that her Spanish was quite good. And then the door of the vehicle swung open, and she was pulled into the coach before she could make a sound. Then it was too late.

In the dark recesses of the carriage, something soft was pushed against her face, then she choked on sweet, sickly fumes. Trying to hold her breath was useless, for her captor had arms of steel, and she couldn't fight away to get a breath of pure air. The fog closed over her, and she knew nothing else until she awakened in the dirty bed, roped into submission, and gagged on a lace-trimmed handkerchief from her own purse. Her head hurt, and her ears were ringing strangely.

The sun had gone down, but a dim oil lamp burned in a ceiling fixture, and she could finally focus her eyes well enough to see two people in the room with her.

The woman who sat on the bed beside her could have been any age from sixteen to thirty-six. The impression given by her too-plentiful makeup and frowzy dress was one of coarseness. Helen had the thought that this could be a very young girl who had lived a very hard and fast life. Her black hair was done up in Spanish style, with a cheap comb which was studded with phoney gems. The gaudy and equally phoney ring on one finger was turning the skin brassy green, and under the hand with the ring, a knee showed pale where a neglected run had opened a black stocking.

The man who had just entered the room was now leaning against the chipped paint of the door. He was maybe an inch taller than Helen's five-eight, and he looked wiry, but not too thin. Helen's first impression was that he could easily be one of the pirates of olden times – or a dancer from one of the Havana cabarets that she'd heard of. The black curls at the front of his brow complemented his olive complexion. He had a gypsy air about him, more pronounced as he flashed white teeth at Helen. He addressed her in Spanish.

"I see you're awake, Miss Longworthy. I hope you are not too uncomfortable." His smile seemed more to mock her than to put her at ease. She tried to speak, but the gag prevented any significant sound from passing her lips, and no one made a move to withdraw it.

"Just as soon as your father delivers a package to a specified place, you will be released near your hotel. Until then, I am very much afraid that your discomfort is necessary to our plans, *Señorita*."

She struggled at her bonds, and tried again to speak. Her eyes were wild with her attempts to communicate. She had to tell them what they couldn't know, before this went on any longer.

Charles Longworthy was an individualist, a man who acted with the courage of his convictions. And if Helen had heard him once state his attitude on kidnapping, she must have heard him a dozen times. Charles Hiram Longworthy II knew his vulnerabilities as a man of wealth who received more publicity than he desired. He took many precautions to lessen the opportunities for those who might wish to victimize him. Helen and Frank had been very closely supervised and guarded, especially in their earlier years. Few temptations and no opportunities were offered to would-be kidnappers.

But Longworthy was adamant about one aspect of this particular crime. He believed that only a fool would comply with a ransom request. It just was not practical for a kidnapper to operate so that the person kidnapped could not recognize him. Inevitably, the criminal would have to consider the possibility of identification and pursuit. So, once he proved that he had the missing victim captive, he would be likely to kill such a witness without further ado.

If he didn't do it then, he would never do it. At any rate, no guarantee ever existed that a kidnap victim would survive after the ransom was paid. Longworthy believed that the only course was to play cat and mouse with the extortionists, calling in the police at the start – or Pinkerton's Detective Agency -- and with no intention of ever paying off.

Right or wrong, Helen knew he wouldn't give in now. His pride as an American was also at stake, here. He wouldn't let any darned spic kidnapper sucker him, no matter what.

Helen continued her struggle to communicate this to her captors. But they ignored her efforts

"My friend still return within the hour. If he brings the money, you are as good as returned to your family. Now, we will go and get something to eat. Come, Consuelo."

They had left her alone, then returned a few minutes later and offered her food. When her gag was removed, she drank a little of the wine they gave her, to moisten her mouth so she could talk.

They laughed at her when she told them what her father's attitude was on kidnapping. They insisted that his talk about the subject would change, now that he was faced with the actuality, rather than the theory. No amount of persuasion could convince them otherwise. Helen was so shaken that she could not eat. They let her relieve herself, Consuelo standing in the small bathroom with her, watching with interest while she urinated, then they tied her to the bed again.

That had been Wednesday, the day they abducted her.

Thursday she remembered with a shudder. Thursday she would always remember! Wednesday night had been unpleasant, especially after the third member of the group returned empty-handed. There had been much loud discussion, most of it arguing, all of it in Spanish. She could hear a little of it through the thin wall, and interpret most of what she heard.

She knew when they had decided to wait until morning before making the next demand. Things had quieted down, and the gypsy-type had stuck his head in the door to give her the word.

"Your foolish father has refused to cooperate so far, just as you predicted. But I believe that tomorrow he will meet our demands, just as I predicted. You see, we are going to send him some pictures of you that should make him wish to end your visit with us. Good night, *Señorita*."

Thursday, though, her real misery had started. It was after she had eaten some fresh bread, and had drunk a cup of surprisingly good *café con leche* – better than the hotel served.

The gypsy-type came into her room, sipping at a cup of the same brew. He watched her as she finished her last bite of bread, and then he spoke to her as he lit a small cigar.

"Today will not be a good day for you, *Señorita* Helen. It will not be a day you will wish to remember. But that is life, of course. One has those days.

"While you were unconscious from the chloroform, we discovered the curious fact of your virginity. No need to blush; it was Consuelo who made the inspection for us. But you will have less privacy from your hosts in the next hours. I suggest that you rest while you can. It is your father who angers me, and I do not wish this to be more difficult for you than necessary."

As if on command, Consuelo removed the breakfast tray from the decrepit dressing table beside the bed, and went out through the doorway to the other room. When she returned, she removed Helen's clothes. All of them. Protest was useless, she knew, so she saved her strength, waiting for what she feared would follow.

Manolo Fernández looked at her appraisingly, and she felt defiled by his inspection. His gaze dwelled overly long on her full, ripe breasts and again on her curly, blonde triangle. "I think that I shall have to sample such a tasty treat before she is spoiled for all time. His dark eyes gleamed greedily, and he met her shocked gaze with insolence.

"It is only just that I derive some pleasure for the trouble I must endure. Is it not so?"

She shuddered, and jumped into the bed, pulling the dirty linen sheet over her, as he laughed shortly, still ogling her, letting his eyes appreciate the soft curves under the stained sheet.

Consuelo sat on the edge of the bed and watched her, as he left the room. Helen's eyes strained to see an avenue of escape. Despite her desperate situation, she was feeling unaccountably sleepy. The window was barred, and she knew it was on the second floor. When she had returned from the bathroom, she had seen that the street below was not busy. She could only spot one pedestrian, a man who fumbled with his fly before turning to relieve himself surreptitiously into the sidewalk gutter.

Maybe they were only threatening her. Trying to get her scared so they could make her tell her father something by telegram, or write him a note. After all, would they really dare to rape an American citizen, one whose family had wealth enough to expend thousands of dollars in vengefully tracking down such criminals?

While she lay there, trying to decide whether to make a wild dash for the window or to resign herself to whatever they might have in store for her, she fell into a sort of uneasy slumber. And when she was awakened, it was too late.

Yes, she would remember Thursday. Her eyes opened, and she saw that Consuelo was gone. The gypsy-type was sitting on the edge of the bed beside her. It had been his hand on her breast that brought her out of her sleep. At the foot of the bed was another man. He was huge, and very black. The descendant of an African slave, probably, she thought. He stood with his arms folded, hands clasped to upper arms. He was a little taller than her father, and must have weighed well over two hundred pounds.

But his face was not as frightening as the gypsy-type's leering countenance. The black seemed not to enjoy his position, even when the other man suddenly whipped back the sheet and exposed her ripe body to view.

"You may have much more meat, Osjami, but this is one of a fine quality, is it not? *Cariño*, eh?" He chuckled to himself, then ran a cool, moist hand over her belly. She shuddered.

They were actually going to do 'it' to her, she realized. And she could never get to the window, now. Then her wrists and ankles were being tied, again. She struggled fiercely, now, but it was too little and too late. The black man was helping, and soon she was spread-eagled once more, this time with her clothes gone.

Then she felt the cool hands on her thighs, moving over the soft skin, tracing upward across her belly, until they reached the full, ripe mounds of her breasts. The hands clutched, one on each proud hemisphere, and she felt a sharp pain as something tiny pricked her.

"Give me your small cigar, Fernández," said the black man. "It will not help to burn her with your ashes."

So that's what felt like a needle; a spark

from his little cigar. She could smell the fragrant blue smoke now. She felt the hand leave her left breast, then return. The black man's footsteps had neared that side of the bed and retreated, as he took the butt from the gypsy. Is his name Manuel? It's so hard to tell Spanish names just from hearing them.

A tremor ran through her as he put his lips on her right breast, nibbling the peak with tantalizing slowness. She felt the nipple distend as it betrayed her, and then his lips were around it, and his wet, warm tongue was flicking at its spongy fullness. She writhed under him, and he chuckled with his mouth full of her breast.

He toyed with her nipples until her breasts ached, and her teeth were clenched in a firm refusal to show any sensual involvement. Then he moved his mouth down her body, trailing his tongue across the sensitive nerve-ends of her belly, dipping it into her navel and swirling it around the little dimple. She arched away from his kiss, but the bedsprings were too old and the mattress too flat to provide any significant distance between them. His avid tongue followed her no matter where she moved.

His mouth had found its way to the blonde forest of her loins. He heard her sharp gasp as his lips nibbled at the edge of the golden jungle, then his tongue found her open slit.

There was no point in trying to close her thighs to him, she reasoned. In any case, her ankles were secured too far apart to give her knees any chance to clamp together. He was enjoying his feast. Little wet sounds slipped past his busy lips as they worked at the pink, moist meat of her vulva. She finally could hold back her tension no longer, and a loud gasp escaped her just as he found her tightening bud with his searching tongue.

Her body arched again – upward this time. Her need had been so magnified by his expert mouth that she reached out for fulfilment. His head was buried in her loins, and again she could hear him as his lips and tongue busily worked her hopelessly exposed vulva.

He's eating my... cunt! Oh, God... that forbidden word! How could I even have thought it! But it feels so wonderful! She couldn't control her thoughts any more than she could control the thrusting of her hips, the shuddering tremors that ran through her body. Ohhh... his mouth is driving me out of my mind!

She felt her hips wiggling from side to side, straining to get the most she could from his hungry mouth, then she was trembling in every part of her body, and she knew she was reaching her pinnacle of passion. The memory of her parents on the quilt by the side of the pool came back to haunt her, a guilty vision.

Suddenly she was her mother, and as Ruth's demands had triggered her climax, so Helen's were now controlling her every sensation. I'm oozing all over the place, and he's drinking it like wine! She felt her last barrier crumble, and she moaned at him, then yelled.

"Oh, Papa! Drink me! Drink me dry!" Then her mind closed as a pink cloudy mist surrounded her, and she felt herself falling, floating downward, endlessly.

She opened her eyes to look into Fernández's face. He was standing beside the bed, and he was now naked. His hard sex was standing rigidly out from his belly, and the wiry black curls at its base seemed coarser than the brown ringlets her father sported in his groin. She was afraid, really afraid, and for the first time, she knew. He was going to pierce her maidenhead, now!

Chapter 2

The Negro was standing at the foot of the bed, and his pink tongue was moistening his lips as he looked down on her ivory body with its nest of golden curls, its two hillocks with pink-tipped peaks. A little trickle of saliva escaped the corner of his mouth and ran down his chin. He wiped at it with a giant hand, not taking his eyes off the vision of beauty.

"Come on, Osjami," said Fernández. "It's time for you to open this lovely package!" She rolled her head on the pillow to look at the smaller man. He was grinning in anticipation at what was going to happen. The black man was naked to the waist when she glanced back at him. He was fumbling with his trousers, then they fell down, taking with them the man's undershorts, if he had been wearing any. For she saw with horror the hugeness and the grandeur of the man, now naked as God had made him. She gave a little moan of terror.

From his dark loins, where a heavy forest of hair was tightly curled, sprouted a fleshy appendage of massive proportions. She imagined the brutal assault that his weapon would make upon her vulnerable sex and grew faint. She had known pain when using a single finger to gratify her own desires, and this was as big around as four fingers, and Lord only knew how long!

"You can't! My God! It will kill me! I'm a virgin – you know that."

Fernández laughed so hard that he bent over almost double.

"Show her, Consuelo," he said, when he caught his breath. Helen hadn't noticed the girl entering the room. Now she saw her standing in the doorway, carrying a wood and brass camera and tripod.

Consuelo strolled calmly over to the foot of the bed where Helen could see easily. Then she lifted a leg and placed it so that the spiked heel of her shoe was against the upper rail of the iron bedstead. Setting down the camera, she used the other hand to lift her skirt high, and Helen could see that the girl wore nothing under it. The stretched thigh pulled at the surrounding tissue, and the dark, heavy lips of the girl's vulva were wide open, showing the pinkness of the parted inner cleft and the vaginal opening. "Go ahead, Osjami," Fernández commanded. The black man moved pivoting on one foot, and laid the meaty, purple head of his weapon against the wet slash of the girl's opening. He shoved slowly in, and Helen watched in horrified fascination as the seemingly normal opening stretched to engulf the gigantic rod. But as the shaft moved in deeper, Consuelo grunted audibly, and her eyes grew large. Her tongue slipped out to moisten suddenly dry lips.

Helen could tell that this girl, who obviously had been stretched before by the same weapon – she had shown no fright when faced with it – yet was affected by its size. If anything, the demonstration had served to add to Helen's fear and horror.

Oh, God! I wanted a cock in me, but not one like that! I think I'd rather stay a virgin forever! She tried to shrink back into the bed, praying for it to swallow her up, to smother her to death. Anything would be preferable to what threatened her now.

Then the black man was kneeling on the bed between her legs. His weapon looked even greater, now, as it neared her. I wanted to take a cock into my mouth, too. But surely, no one could take *this* in their mouth! Fernández had pulled the pillow from under her head, and now he forced it under her hips, doubled, making them tilt upwards toward the black invader that was poised over her quivering belly.

She was vaguely aware of Consuelo moving nearer, aiming the camera at the bed, then a flash as the little tray of magnesium

powder ignited a split second before the shutter clicked. Thank God! Maybe they only need the horror of a shot like this to shock Papa Longworthy into changing his mind. But somehow she knew, even as the thought came, that she wasn't to get off that easily.

The tip of the hard shaft was lying in the cleft of her moist canyon, and a face hovered close her own as the black man leaned down to speak to her.

"I tell you this to help you, *Señorita* Helen. It will not be as difficult for you if you try to want me. Try to wish this thing inside of you. Your body will not fight it as much, and you will have less damage. Understand?" He looked into her eyes, and she could tell that he was not in favour of causing her pain. His brown eyes seemed to reflect a pain of his own.

"*Si, yo entiendo. Gracias.*" She acknowledged with thanks. Perhaps he could lessen the pain.

Then it had begun. Oh, Lord! How it had begun!

It felt as though she was being torn asunder in a hundred different directions. They could have achieved the same feeling by thrusting a spear inside her, she imagined. Then she realized she was fighting it, and tried to reverse her muscles. It was impossible. To get to the point where she could will the damned thing to be inside her, she would first have to relax. My God, I can't relax when I'm being torn apart!

Then the black hands were on her breasts, caressing them, kneading the nipples to full erection, gently massaging their pink rubbery tips between dark brown fingers. She felt herself tingling, becoming impassioned in spite of the pain, and then his hands were squeezing both nipples firmly, and she started to moan her pleasure.

The burning sensation just inside the entrance to her tender passage had not increased, but it was a constant reminder. Like a camel straining to get through the eye of the needle, she thought, dimly. She needed air; she threw her head back and gulped some into her lungs. Then the kneading hands were replaced by the moistness of a hot mouth, and she felt nipple, aureole, and a large part of the firm mound itself being drawn into the hungry, warm, wet mouth.

She gasped at the sensation, and her throat opened to moan her surprised delight. Then she felt the ripping-tearing-spreading pain of the fleshy cock boring into her tender depths

It's tearing my cunt apart! It's plunging right into my guts like a giant knife. She almost couldn't bear the pain, but as she started to pass out, she felt the delicious sensation of his massaging lips and tongue on her breasts, and her senses seemed to slow just a second to savour the feeling. Then the pain in her depths lessened, her panic receded, and she thought she might just be able to endure the ordeal.

Until the pulsing started. The head of the big shaft was now pressing snugly against her innermost defences, and when it swelled within her, stretching the tender passage in throbbing pulses, she thought she was going to be sick. The hurtful spasms brought her to the borderline of extreme nausea several times, and then perversely, it began to feel almost good.

Her body was moving without her willing it to motion; the suction of the hungry mouth on her breast and the pressure of the black padded pelvis against her hard, wet bud carried her past the pain of the gross invader's violation. Her hips thrust upward, and she could feel the rope tension on her ankles as her heels sank into the bed. The black man began to stroke into her depths, pulling the now slippery shaft almost out of its fleshy scabbard, then sinking it again to the hilt. Helen could feel the man's big scrotal sac as it flopped with a wet smack against her buttocks and crotch. The tingling tremors that were running through her body carried her back once more to the night by the garden pool, and her passion awoke the memory of that dark night as the black flesh plunged into her.

"Fuck me deep, Papa! Stick it in hard! My poor little pussy is starved! " She heard her own voice with surprise, and it shocked her, but the intensity of her feelings was so great she couldn't control herself. As it became even more intense, she heard herself cry out again.

"Squirt it in me! Now! Ohhhh!" Then the roller coaster took her up, up, clear to the top of an unbelievable peak, and as she started to fall, she felt the pumping, squirting streams of warm liquid splash into the tender walls of her being.

She fell a long way, and then floated softly on a cloud. When she opened her eyes, the black man was leaning back from her, and the black flesh of his rod was retreating from her passage. As it came all the way out, she watched the purplish head appear, trailing strings of white, sticky semen behind it.

The side of the dark sword were streaked with blood, and she knew why as the burning sensation returned to her torn tissues. Her breathing was a laboured panting, and it seemed as if she'd never get enough air. She gasped deeply, and felt her lungs start to fill normally again.

The dark lance was bent, curving

downward in a tired arc, the purple head resting on the sheet in a little pool of liquid white that gleamed in the morning sun that came through the barred window.

"Consuelo! Make Osjami ready again!" Fernández commanded.

The brunette had been doing something at the dresser. When she moved away from it, Helen could see several exposed plates lying on top of the dirty wood. The girl came over to the bed and kneeled on the edge, then leaned over Helen's thigh and placed her mouth on the black shaft. With a sideways movement of her head, she stroked the dark length, using lips and tongue, until the dormant rod began to stir slightly.

When the purplish-red glans lifted off the sheet, Consuelo took it into her mouth and began to rotate her head, working the fleshy tip between her teeth, then snaking out her tongue to lash around the coronal ridge, first clockwise, then counter clockwise. Helen, hearing the wet sounds as Consuelo sucked in the remnants of semen, felt truly nauseous. Then the tongue slipped down and stroked the side of the shaft again, cleaning off the streaks of white and red from the dark skin.

Helen fought to keep from getting sick. She knew she would get herself covered with it, and have to lie in it. She forced herself to think of other things, but then she saw the great shaft swell into its former size and hardness, and Consuelo gave it a last sucking tug, then slid off the bed.

Osjami leaned over her, and the big meaty stick lay snugly in the canyon formed by the swollen lips of her sex. His mouth again sought her breasts. Soon she was inescapably caught up in her passion once more. He was moving the hardness slowly against her hypersensitive surfaces while his hands and mouth worked at her breasts.

She began to moan and move under him, as the burning sensation was gradually dwarfed by the mounting feelings from within. Then both hands were on her breasts, and the black man's lips were pressed to hers.

As her lips opened to gasp, his tongue entered and plunged around inside, teasing her lips and toying with her tongue, until she could not remain passive her pink tongue pushed out to fence with his, and he drank deeply of her warm, sweet juices, then sucked her hot tongue until she shivered in ecstasy.

He leaned away from her, and then the head of his lance was at the opening of her torn passage. He thrust it inside slowly, until it filled her completely. Then he resumed with long, heavy strokes that drove her wild. His mouth moved over to her shoulder, where he nibbled and sucked at the tender flesh.

There was a sinking of the bed near her

head, and she glanced away from passion-swollen eyes to see Fernández kneeling by her face. He was as naked as Osjami, and he held his own erect member in his hand. She watched as the swollen head of his tan cock came towards her, then it was against her lips

"Take this! You watched Consuelo. Now do the same!" He pressed the bulging glans of his penis between her lips before she could turn away from it. Then it was in her mouth!

She almost gagged, but the things Osjami was doing to her had her in a passionate trance, and she closed her lips over the hard-soft thing and soon found herself tonguing it in a rotation that drew groans from Fernández's throat.

He pushed the shaft further into her mouth, until it touched the back of her throat, then yelled to Consuelo.

"Cut the ropes, Consuelo! Quick!" In a few moments, Helen felt her ankles and wrists freed, but instead of struggling, she was amazed to find that her legs were wrapping around the black man, and that she had grasped Fernández's shaft with one hand, and was using the other to massage the soft bag of his scrotum.

Then the movements grew swifter, as the dark invader below and the white one above plunged into her deeply. She was thankful for the free hand which encircled Fernández's tool, keeping it from choking her completely. Then she trembled throughout her body, and her hips arched upward, pushing back against the black man's thrusts, and clinging around him, frantically gripping with her legs.

Her mouth began to move on the flesh it held, stroking it in hungry grabs. As she felt herself soaring upward in uncontrollable ecstasy, she felt the throbbing pulsations of the meaty mouthful, and suddenly Fernández's grunting sounds were marking time with the spurts of his seed against the back of her throat. She swallowed heavily, and managed not to choke.

Then the black man was moaning and humming his release, and the pumping of his spurting liquid inside her tender vaginal passage marked the end of her climb. Her persecutors left the hot, airless room and Helen fell back, exhausted.

* * *

As she recalled the degradation of the Thursday morning orgy, she felt more violated than she had when it occurred. She could still feet the sticky strings of semen on her cheek, as though she had just now awakened from the sleep which followed the assault.

That had been only yesterday. And most of that afternoon and all of last night, she had slept, exhausted. Her young body was mending itself, she felt. But the lack of food since that shocking extent, and the shame she felt as she thought about those photos being seen by her family, made her feel sick all over.

She jerked to chase away the flies, again. Then the door opened and Fernández and Consuelo entered. They removed the gag from her mouth and the swarthy man addressed her.

"You are going to join your family. If you promise to be quiet and cooperate, we will not replace this handkerchief in your mouth. Do you promise to do as you are told?"

Helen's mouth was too dry to speak, but she nodded. Consuelo brought her a drink of water, and she held the first sip in her mouth a moment, then swallowed painfully. Soon she was gulping down the entire glassful, hoping that it had been purified by boiling. Surely they knew about typhoid and such, she thought.

They untied the ropes, and helped her up. She moved slowly to the bathroom on wobbly legs, leaning on Consuelo's arm all the way. After relieving herself, she tried to clean up a little. There was no washcloth, but she did the best she could. There was a bidet in the

room, and she managed to douche herself satisfactorily, though the clear water burned in numerous areas, as the protecting film of lubricant was rinsed away.

They blindfolded her, and led her down a rickety staircase. She was helped into a coach, and heard the doors close. Then they were moving, the metal wheels clattering over cobblestones. The trip seemed endless. Finally, she began to get frightened. Were they really taking her somewhere to kill her?

"Where are we going? We've travelled long enough to drive clear across Havana several times." There was a sob in her voice. She put her hands over her face, out of habit, as she started to cry under the blindfold.

"Do not worry, little one. Your family is no longer at the hotel where you left them. We are going to a different place, and you will see them soon."

As one part of her mind absorbed this consolation, another part worked on his phrasing. It see-sawed between the ordeal being over and – being about to begin in earnest. How could they be taking her to her family, surrounded by policemen, as they must surely be?

She knew that Fernández sat on her left, and even if occasional bumps in the bad road had not thrown her arm against Consuelo's breast, Helen would have known the brunette sat on her right, if only from the odour. This woman was a living example of the legend about the Spanish use of perfume as a substitute for bathing. Yet, it wasn't all legend, she knew. In the days when bathing was considered detrimental to the health, even by the medical profession, scents were developed to mask the strong body smells. But there was no excuse for it in the twentieth century!

She realized with a little thrill that when her hands had been pressed to her face, part of her blindfold had been shifted, and a small slit of light was in her eyes. She hoped it hadn't been noticed. Stealthily, she moved her head about, pretending to relieve a stiff neck, adding to the effect by massaging it with her hands as she turned it.

Suddenly she caught a glimpse of a road sign ahead. She tried to memorize what she had seen, but they passed it very quickly. Her mind worked at it, trying to be sure what she had seen. Was it Cabañas 35 kilometers, Artemisa 32 kilometers? Or what was the other name and figure? San Cristobal or something? She didn't know. Maybe the little bit she thought she had seen would be of value later.

She tried to get an occasional glimpse of the scenery, looking for usable landmarks, thanking her special Providence that the thin material was coarsely woven, enabling her to distinguish quite a bit through its screening.

She guessed that Osjami was driving the coach. She could hear the snort of the horses, and occasionally, the clinking sound of bridle and bit.

Then she began to see people on horseback, and an occasional cart or coach coming from the opposite direction. Suddenly they were in a small town; she saw something which almost made her gasp. She stopped her reaction just before they would have heard her sharp intake of breath.

There before her, definitely recognizable from a photograph in Papa Longworthy's wartime album, was a building which had been called, in 1898, Hall of the States. She could remember the signs from the photo; signs which ran around the upper part of the lower-floor facade, each with the name of a state. It had been a sort of service club for troops in the area.

Her heart pounded with the recognition. She had figured out that if she were blindfolded, it had to be because of some advantage she would acquire by knowing the route they took. So she had made some headway without their knowing it.

The big coach took off on an oblique angle, down a street which soon became another semi-improved road. They rode for several miles before the coach slowed, then turned up a lane between long hedgerows, and approached a big stone farmhouse. They stopped in front of the large door, and Osjami got down and opened the door. Fernández got out, and reached inside, taking Helen's hand to guide her out.

Soon they were inside the building, and when the door closed, Helen's blindfold was removed. She made a great fuss over blinking and rubbing around her eyes, elaborating on her deception.

Then she was taken to a door at the back of the house, and as it opened, she saw steps leading down into a cellar. Fernández went ahead of her, and Osjami followed behind, as they descended the wooden stairs. Fernández stopped at the bottom, and turned on a switch. As the place filled with light, Helen's breath caught in a gasping sob. The walls of the cellar were of the same heavy stone as the rest of the farmhouse. And along two walls of this dismal, dungeon-like place, shackles were fastened to the stones with huge iron rings. She saw the three figures shackled to the cruel chains, and cried heartbrokenly as she ran toward them.

"Papa Longworthy!" she sobbed, throwing her arms about the nearest prisoner. She looked up into his face, and his eyes were full of his mental agony. His face had a beaten look.

She left him in confusion and ran to her

mother, who was chained on the adjoining wall, hugging the limply hanging body, which came tensely alive under her daughter's embrace. The two sobbed in unison at their plight, then Helen reached over and squeezed Frank's hand above its manacled wrist, right next to Ruth's position on the wall.

Helen whirled to their captors with the fire of anger in her blue eyes. She almost spit out her words at them.

"What do you scoundrels think you are doing? You'll never get any money this way!" She was so full of her hate that she couldn't say another word, but just stood there, seething. She didn't even realize that she had spoken to them in English, until Fernández answered.

"You have been treated with more gentleness than we ordinarily use, because you have spoken to us in the language of our country. Now, it seems, you have reverted to the ugly American, which makes it easier for us to proceed with out next move.

"You see, your greedy father would not part with money, even after he saw the pictures of your little adventure. Now, we shall at least have some entertainment for our troubles. Osjami! Chain her!" She felt the huge hands as they grasped her wrists, and she was taken to the wall and shackled next to her father. Then their captors went up the steps, dimming the light, and left them alone to their misery.

Chapter 3

The closing of the heavy door at the top of the steps had a discouragingly final sound. The captives were silent for several minutes, as each reflected upon their fate. Not knowing what was in store for them, their fears multiplied, their imaginations working overtime. To add to their mental misery, their physical discomforts were acute.

The chains to which they were shackled permitted just enough freedom to allow them a choice of standing or sitting. And the cuffs at their ankles and wrists were snug enough to prevent escape, yet moved freely in place, guaranteeing them additional discomfort as the friction chafed their skin.

Helen's whereabouts had been a mystery to her family, but they had known that she was a captive. But the appearance of her family here was a great shock to her, and her lack of comprehension moved her to speak while the others were still lost in their own miserable thoughts and imaginings.

"What happened? How did they get their hands on all of you, anyhow?" She was even more frightened when only silence greeted her questions. "Tell me! For God's sake! Someone say something!" She almost started to break down and cry anew, when her father broke the silence of the dark dungeon with his reply.

"Late last night, someone left an envelope at the door to our suite, rang the buzzer, and left. When I opened it, there was a note inside, and ... and ... those pictures of you ... I guess you didn't have any choice ... you were tied up in all of them except one ... and maybe they had you drugged, too ..." She could sense the questioning tone as he referred to the final picture Consuelo had taken. She'd barely been aware of the final flash and click of that spying shutter, because she'd been occupied with the two men invading her body.

Oh, God! He's thinking about the picture where my arms and legs are free. What was I doing? Oh, no! My legs were wound around Osjami, and I was working on Fernández's cock with my mouth and both hands! It's better if he thinks I was drugged when that picture was taken. And perhaps I was.

"The note said that this was the last chance to pay, unless I wanted even more horrible things to happen." Charlie Longworthy's tone made his daughter feel as if she had let him down by not answering his unspoken question, but she knew it was better to ignore the issue now. There were enough problems here without breaking his heart. And she sensed that he'd never get over it if he discovered that she had enjoyed any part of that degrading assault.

"I guess you know, Helen, that I just couldn't cooperate with kidnappers, no matter how worried we were about you." The question was back in his voice, and this time she knew that she had to answer, to set his mind at ease. He was miserable enough without having to doubt whether Helen forgave him for not ransoming her.

"I know, Papa Longworthy. I tried to tell them, but I couldn't get them to listen to me. I know how you feel about kidnapping, and I knew from the first they wouldn't collect, so I didn't have any false hopes shattered. I may not agree with your opinions on the subject one hundred percent, but I'm proud that you stuck to your guns and left them hanging high and dry without the money. But that doesn't explain how they grabbed all of you."

"I'm not so proud of myself, right now. If I'd sacrificed my personal convictions, even if you might not have been freed, at least your mother and brother wouldn't have had to go through whatever it is they've got planned for us. But it's too late to cry over it, now.

"I delivered a package as they requested, but instead of the ransom, I wrapped a note in heavy cardboard. The note told them that I had not and would not change my mind. And that if any harm came to you, I'd spend several million dollars and the rest of my natural life in hunting them down and killing them." He heaved a hoarse sigh which sounded even more rasping than the dry-throated voice he spoke to her with. Helen wondered when he'd last had a drink of water.

"It might have worked with a professional of normal mentality, Papa, but this Fernández is mad. And the others will do anything he tells them to do. Lord knows what he's cooking up for us in that evil mind. If only ..." She stopped speaking suddenly, as she had an idea. "If only what, honey?" Longworthy asked.

"Papa, do you have any idea whether we're being overheard or not?" She felt overly melodramatic as she asked the question, but their future might depend on it.

"I'd thought of that, too. But I don't know if ..." Now it was Helen's turn to wonder about an unfinished "if" statement. But she waited to see what he had in mind. Suddenly she knew, as she heard him speak again, and she had all she could do to keep from laughing her delight at his quick wit.

"I want you all to know that I have a plan in mind," Longworthy announced, raising the volume of his cracked voice, as though trying to be sure all of the family could hear him. "When they searched me, they overlooked the knife I have strapped to my leg. The first time one of them gives me the least chance, I'll sink it in as deep as I can!"

"That's great, Papa Longworthy!" said Helen, faking it along with him smoothly. "They don't know they're up against an ex-Rough Rider."

"Good for you, Pater!" chimed in Frank, as he sized up the idea his father had begun to put into use. "Charlie, I've asked you a hundred times not to carry any kind of weapon. It only leads to trouble." Even Ruth Longworthy had seized on her husband's brilliant strategy to find out if they were being listened to.

They all fell silent for a while, as if waiting to see whether the bait would be taken Then Longworthy realized the silence itself would betray them.

"I hope it's that damned Fernández who gets near me," he continued. "I'd love to feel a knife slipping into his sadistic guts!"

"And I'd love to see his insides spread out on the floor, too" replied Helen, not having to fake the hatred she felt for the sadist.

"Me, too," Frank added. "But make sure he's got a key to these cuffs before you do it!"

"You shouldn't talk like that!" said Ruth. "It puts you in the same class with ..."

The door at the top of the stairs opened, and a dim light was reflected down against the opposite wall of the cellar. As the sound of someone descending the steps fell on their ears, all of them felt that their plan had born fruit, and that their captors could indeed hear what they were saying in the cellar.

The light at the foot of the stairs was lit, and their eyes blinked as they adjusted to the sudden illumination. Then they saw Fernández moving across the basement floor toward them. He was carrying an earthenware pitcher and cups. He stopped beside Helen.

"We want our guests to be in good enough condition to provide us with satisfactory entertainment. Here, *Señorita*. *Para usted*.

He poured a stream into one of the cups, then handed it to her. As she sipped, cautiously, she discovered that it was rum and water.

Fernández moved down the line, stopping next to give Longworthy one of the cups, then pouring it full of the diluted rum. His casual behaviour as he stood close to the tycoon convinced everyone that he had not heard the phoney boast about the knife.

As Longworthy sipped at the drink, letting it flow around his dry mouth and throat, Fernández moved to the wall where Ruth and Frank were licking their lips in anticipation. When he had given each of them a drink, he moved toward the centre of the basement as if heading back toward the stairs, then turned to face them. He looked with deliberation at the captives chained to the two walls, from his vantage point almost directly out from the corner.

He's standing on the hypotenuse of our family triangle, Helen thought, realizing her silliness even as she thought it. This drink must be drugged! What are they planning to do?

"In a few minutes, we will bring you something to eat. When the food has had a chance to digest, then we will begin our little circus. Will that not be nice? *El Circo* Fernández, it may not get to become famous on the island, but here in... here among our exclusive company, we shall have much amusement.

"Perhaps you may feel a little strange from your drink. It is not the rum of your American bar stock. It is genuine local variety, and has somewhat more strength from the sugar cane. Is it not so?"

Fernández laughed to himself, as he turned away and went back up the stairs, leaving the light on, this time. When the door closed, Helen looked at her father, and his gaze met hers with a quiet recognition of their victory in the test operation to see if they were being overheard.

"Did you notice that he still doesn't

want us to know where we are??' asked Longworthy. "That can only be due to the fact that he expects us to live to tell about it. He doesn't intend to kill us, then. At least we learned that much." His eyes glinted with the realization that they had won a small battle.

"Brace yourself, Papa Longworthy," said Helen. "I know where we are. At least, I think I can help you figure it out pretty closely."

"What do you mean, honey? Weren't you blindfolded on the way here, like we were?" He watched the elfin grin creep across his daughter's mouth and cheek.

"Yes, but it was pretty coarse material, and in one spot-a very convenient spot-it was only a single thickness, and I could see through it. We're just a little way from the centre of Cabañas, Papa. Remember the Hall of States in that photograph?"

"Yes, yes, honey. But, don't tell me that's still there like it was."

"No, Papa. The signs aren't there, but it's the same building; the very same place. And as we came into town from Havana, we turned left there in front of the place, and I recognized it."

"Thank God! What a stroke of luck. Let's see. If only I can remember after all these years. What was it out that direction?" Longworthy closed his eyes as he strained to recall the topography out of his past. Helen watched his knuckles turn white as his hands clenched in desperate tension to match his mental pressures.

"Very well. I think I've got it! Now, did you make any other turns?"

"No. I don't think so. We kept going until we came to the lane that leads up to this house."

"How far are we from the Hall of States. That's very important."

"I think it must be about four or five miles. One thing I'm sure of: right out front, as you turn into the lane, there is a hedgerow on either side of the lane. And to the left of the lane, there is a small plantation of bananas. Right down through the centre of the plantation, three rows have been harvested. There are bananas in all the other rows or there were when I saw it."

"Good show, Helen, honey! We mustn't let them know that we have the least idea where we are. It could mean our deaths, all of us."

"I've been thinking about something else," Helen said, wondering how to describe what she had in mind while the whole family was listening, hanging on her every word. Then she shrugged, and jumped right into it.

"Every little thing we can arrange to throw them off stride, even the smallest bit, will work in our favour. Isn't that what you used to tell us about your army training, Papa Longworthy?"

"That's right, sweetheart. Hard to tell how much good it will do us in this case, but you never know. What do you have in mind?"

"They let me keep my purse, after they took out my nail file and a few other things. I see that Mother has her purse, too. The thought just came to me that there is no identification on the little leather case that Doctor Vaughn gave to us. It contains all the equipment necessary. And Mother could use it each time, too."

"What equipment is that, honey?" Longworthy's brow wrinkled as he tried to imagine what his daughter was taking that he knew nothing about.

"Prophylactic equipment for ladies," Helen mumbled. She felt the flush move upward from her neck, and her face grew warm. Ruth came to her rescue.

"It's something I thought Helen should use, just in case she got carried away by her female emotions on a heavy date, dear. We girls sometimes refer to them as 'just-in-cases' when we really don't expect to require the immunity they provide."

"Kee-rist! What's our younger generation going to come to? If parents provide them with sponges and douches and what-have-you, they can live like the latter Greeks."

Longworthy turned to his daughter. "Have you been using those things so you could give yourself to some guy whenever you got the hots for him?" Helen sensed the protective jealousy emanating from her father. His face was almost livid.

"Of course not! It's just as Mother told you. Using them is the same as getting all those inoculation injections when you leave the States. You don't really plan to expose yourself to typhus and plague, and all that, Father, now do you? But if something happens … unexpectedly, beyond your control, you have some protection."

Longworthy didn't need the disgust in Helen's tone to tell him he'd goofed with his outburst. She never called him 'Father' unless she was really miffed with him. He turned and looked at his wife, as if she could help him take his foot out of his mouth.

"Don't look to me for moral support," Ruth told him. "You ought to know your daughter's character better than that. Make your own explanations and apologies."

Longworthy's face was pink as he turned back to Helen. He sputtered a little, but he managed to apologize satisfactorily, as Helen's relaxing features told him. But at her next words, he paled.

"If I have any free guesses, it might just be a good idea for us to use those things.

Fernández has a one-track mind when it comes to entertainment "

"You did mention giving your mother a sponge, too. Do you think that they ... I mean, you don't really believe that they intend to ... for the love of God, child, you don't think that ... Yes, I can see that you do."

The rum and water was beginning to make Longworthy sweat. Beads of perspiration were starting to roll down into his eyes. He looked at Ruth, then at his daughter, then back at Frank, who had remained silent during the sex-oriented discussion.

Longworthy's eyes looked haunted, and Helen thought that he seemed to age several years in a few seconds. She felt a surge of maternal protectiveness for this father whose selective naïveté could render him into a small boy in his unsophisticated moments. She attempted to detour his train of thought.

"I still haven't heard how they captured you." Longworthy's eyes responded, and he appeared to straighten slightly as he changed his leaning position against the stone wall.

"After I'd sent them that note, we stayed in the hotel suite for several hours. Then it seemed a good idea to check in at the Consulate, again. So we all went over there, and talked to the same attaché I'd given the original report to. He'd been in constant touch with the *policía*, and they had just turned in a negative report for the dozenth time, explaining that none of their informers seemed to have any knowledge of the kidnapping.

"We spent almost two hours there, hoping that the Consul General would get back from the US mainland, and be able to trigger more action. Finally, we started walking back to the hotel. I was too nervous to ride in one of those cabs.

"Several blocks from the hotel, a coach pulled up, and Fernández got out and walked up to me. He said that he had been asked to take us to pick you up. We all crowded around the cab, and he grabbed your mother and pulled her inside, where he held a gun on her to force Frank and me to cooperate. He kept the gun on Ruth until we pulled up in an alley, where he and Osjami blindfolded us. All the time, he kept insisting that he was bringing us to meet you, but couldn't let us know where the meeting place was.

"We thought it was perhaps some more pressure; that they would let us see you in some sort of miserable condition, thinking that I would give in and pay them. But their note obviously meant what it said-they'd already given me the last chance to pay." Longworthy's voice almost broke as he implied his failure to handle the situation properly.

"Like you said, Papa – they seem to intend for us to leave here alive. Whatever else happens, we'll just have to bear up under it."

Longworthy had no chance to reply to this. The door at the top of the stairs opened, and all three of their captors descended, carrying trays of food. Consuelo was her same, seemingly unemotional self, and Osjami appeared only to be concerned with his duties as waiter. But Fernández was smiling evilly, and Helen knew he was anticipating the "entertainment" he'd mentioned. She shuddered as she tried to eat the first bites of the dish before her.

Trays balanced on their knees as they squatted, all four of the captives started their meal slowly, but hunger hastened their moves. The meal of pork, rice and beans was actually quite palatable, although at this point, none of them really enjoyed it.

When the trays were gathered up, Fernández withdrew with his companions, but as he reached the middle of the stairway, he turned his head and addressed the unhappy family over his shoulder.

"The fun starts in two hours. I'll leave you to think about it as your meal settles. *Hasta luego!*"

It seemed much less than two hours between Fernández's mocking departure and his return. But Longworthy knew that the Cuban's timing was precise; because their captors had permitted the family to keep their timepieces, Longworthy had been able to check the big pocket watch he always carried.

During that compressed two-hour interlude, considerable conversation had accomplished only one thing for the prisoners. Discussing their predicament had lessened its effects. The feeling of togetherness, the sharing of the burden, made it easier. Helen felt this more strongly, since she had suffered the only solitary confinement. Now, there was hope that, combining their capabilities, they might be able to figure ways to escape.

But before any specific ideas came to light, they were interrupted by Fernández's appearance. Osjami was with him. The pair descended the stairs and approached the wall occupied by Longworthy and Helen.

"We shall establish some basic facts before we go any further," Fernández told them. He was gazing into Longworthy's eyes, but both he and his audience of four knew it concerned them all.

"Any and all attempts to escape will result in punishment. You have my guarantee that no matter what you imagine, your punishment will more than compensate me for any trouble you cause. You will be wise to believe this and guide your behaviour accordingly.

"Non-cooperation also will be punished.

Certain things will be asked – no, *demanded* of each of you. You will comply with every request; obey every command; accomplish everything you are told to do. Each and every failure will result in punishment. Hesitation, if it is enough to provoke me, will merit the same punishment as a refusal. Now, are there any doubts that I mean what I say?"

He looked at each of the captives in turn, and as their eyes met the sadistic evil that glinted in his dark orbs, they accepted his statements without question.

"Take *Señor* Longworthy upstairs, Osjami."

Fernández's words were barely uttered when the black man inserted a key in Longworthy's ankle cuffs. When these shackles were released, he unlocked the cuffs on the prisoner's wrists. Then he walked to the stairs and began to ascend. Osjami followed him at a safe distance. When he reached the top of the steps, he found himself in a large old kitchen. Consuelo was standing by the opposite wall, and the small but efficient-looking revolver she held was aimed at his stomach.

He was herded through the kitchen and a connecting room, which probably was a dining room, but which was now unfurnished. Then he was guided through a hall and into a large, ground-floor bedroom. It was furnished only with a large double bed and two chairs.

"Remove all your clothes," said Consuelo, who had followed him as far as the doorway, and continued to level the gun in his direction. He looked at her sharply, but decided against argument. He undressed down to his undershirt and shorts.

"I said 'all your clothes' and that means everything!" Her tone advised him against hesitation. He finished, and stood there naked, glumly eying the neat pile of clothes he'd made on one of the two occasional chairs. His shoes and socks were on the floor beside the chair. A casual observer arriving now would give him credit for his neatness. Consuelo grinned at this orderly display. Such behaviour was not typical of her customers.

"Inside!" Fernández's voice came from the hall. Longworthy turned to see his daughter being shoved into the bedroom. She had seen her father's nudity, and was keeping her eyes averted. He grabbed his shorts from the chair and held them in front of his groin.

"Forget the modesty, Mr. Longworthy. In a few minutes, you will be more familiar with your daughter than you have been since she was an infant – and she with you. Off with your clothes, Helen!"

The girl heaved a sigh of resignation, then slowly began to remove her blouse. In a few minutes, she had used the other chair to arrange a pile of clothing as neat as her that of her father.

"*Bien!* Now, on the bed – both of you!" Fernández's voice was like a whip. Longworthy looked at him unbelievingly, and couldn't contain his anger and shock.

"You must be mad! What in the name of God are you thinking of?"

"You do not believe that, Mr. Longworthy. Surely you are intelligent enough to know that you must humour a madman in his every whim. But I am a fanatic about being obeyed. You will cause no further delay, or you will see your daughter suffer for your folly! Now, get in bed with her. Immediately!"

Longworthy sat on the bed, noting that Helen already had complied.

"Lie down, and embrace each other as lovers. Quickly!"

Longworthy's shocked mind couldn't convince him that this was actually happening. Certainly Fernández was bluffing. No one could expect him to comply with such a monstrous command! He looked up at the Cuban in disbelief, and the expression on Fernández's face told him what he dared not accept.

"*Señor* Longworthy, perhaps we can speed things up if I explain one more thing to you. I intend to turn you loose to permit you to gather up the ransom money, which now, by the way, has doubled, because of the additional trouble you've caused us.

"Naturally, I will expect you not to return here with the authorities. First, you do not know where we are; you will be released at a safe place in Havana, and you will return there with the money. Second, I am going to have some photographs of your entire family – photographs which I am sure you will not want to see fall into the wrong hands – in fact, I think that you will very much want to destroy these pictures.

"Now, if you do as you are told, we will take the pictures, and you will go to get the money. When you return, and we wait a while to be sure that you have not been followed, we will take the money, let you burn the pictures, then release all of you. Do you not see the beauty and simplicity of my plan?"

"But ... but ... there must be some other kind of blackmail you can work. This ... this ... incestuous thing you imply is too ... too grotesque to be rational. I beg of you ..."

"No. There will be no changes in my plans. This type of photo I know you will be anxious to recover. Therefore, I am confident in the value of the plan. Now, do not waste any more time, or your lovely daughter will suffer for your hardness of head. Move!"

Longworthy, shaken terribly, turned to his daughter. As he lay beside her, he whispered his misery and hopeless helplessness to her. As he put his arms around her, he hoped that she could keep her young mind from being affected by this terrible trauma.

"Helen, baby. Forgive me for having gotten you into such a terrible situation. I don't think we have any choice, if he means what he says." He felt her tender young body tremble under his embrace.

"You couldn't help it, Papa Longworthy. Don't blame yourself. And he does mean everything he says. I know it! We'll have to do just what we're told, and try not to let it get us down."

"You're a great sport, honey. I've always known that, I guess. But I never would have believed that you'd be forced to prove it like this!"

"Enough tenderness! Let us now have some real poses. Consuelo! Over here with the camera!" The sleazy prostitute moved around the bed until she had a good view of the models.

"Very well. *Señor* Longworthy, place your left hand on Helen's right hip, and take her breast in your mouth."

Longworthy's eyes were full of pain as he slowly started to respond. Helen flashed him a look of compassion, then closed her eyes as she spoke.

"Go ahead, Papa Longworthy. The better

we cooperate, the sooner it will be over."

He felt the warm, young flesh under his fingers, and it stirred him, in spite of his horror at the immorality of the thing. And as his lips touched her firm, virginal breasts, he knew again the thrill that had run through him the first time he'd kissed Ruth's tender globes. The springy nipple which blossomed under his oral caress popped between his lips, and he squeezed it in passionate reflex before he realized what he was doing.

"Take his *pinga*, his cock, in your hand, Helen. Hurry up!" ordered Fernández.

She gingerly reached down between them and found his semi-soft member. As her fingers moved through his wiry thatch and encountered their target, Helen felt a tingling tremor course through her. The forbidden nature of the act they were forced into made it even more exciting than she would have believed. In spite of her initial inner decision to remain aloof as she complied with Fernández's commands, she couldn't prevent the triggering of her libido.

It called back to her in vivid imagery the scene by the ornamental pool at home. The lusty member she had envied her mother's possessing was now in her grasp. She squeezed it gently, revelling in the erotic feel of his hardening length. A tiny moan escaped her lips.

"Now, Longworthy, you repay her kindness

by caressing her little pussy, her little *chocha*, as we call it here."

His tone revealed his enjoyment of directing them in this obscene piece of sexual theatre.

Longworthy tried. He honestly strained to force his hand into the forbidden forest of his daughter's genital area. But the knowledge of what he was about to do was too much for his years of prescribed morality, and his hand jerked back the moment it touched her golden feathers.

"I can't do it! I just can't!" he groaned, hating himself for his helplessness, caught between the inevitable hammer of the physical torture threatening Helen, and the immovable anvil of his innate psychic block.

Fernández had lit a small cigar as Longworthy's hand reneged. Now, the Cuban blew on the glowing tip, and swiftly pressed it against the girl's buttock. She screamed her pain and outrage as the tender flesh blistered.

"From this point on," promised Fernández, "it will be the face which is burned. Perhaps even some surgery will be required." The tortured look in Longworthy's eyes underwent a change. The indecision was gone, and in its place was beaten resignation.

His hand moved into the golden curls of his daughter's most private area, and he felt the slippery wetness exuded by the inner lips Her thighs separated to receive his attentions, and his fingertips fell on her surprisingly swollen little bud. Her hips moved to help him get started, and soon he was providing the massage motions, with only an occasional thrust of her agile young hips.

"Take my breast in your mouth, again," Helen whispered. Longworthy, taking it for a warning against not being cooperative enough, hastened to comply. His lips found the firm mound, and trailed up its satin slope to the pink-capped peak, and seized the spongy blossom. His tongue automatically toyed with the delicious morsel, and Helen's humming sound was a familiar melody, so much like Ruth's responses.

The performers were dimly aware of snapping-shutter sounds, and the flashes caused by the magnesium powder. But they began to be carried away by their treacherous sexualities.

Helen's hand was moving, slowly, gently milking the fleshy lance in her grasp, and Longworthy's heavy breathing started to be interspersed with mild groans, as his passion increased.

The girl's lubricious flow was wetting Longworthy's fingers, and he used it expertly to continually oil her erect little bud, as he caressed its tender surface. Her legs opened wider to him, and she manoeuvred her hips to capture a finger in the swelling softness of her melting passage. As it entered her, the thumb took over the massage duties of the upper area, and her excitement increased.

She turned toward him more, and with her free hand moved his head to place the delightful suction on the neglected breast.

As his finger probed her flowing depths, the tender morsel of her nipple quivered under his tasting tongue, Longworthy lost himself completely in the remembered lusts of his youth. It was the young Ruth whose body he now possessed, so firmly but softly yielding to his assault. And the girl's nymph-like responses to his every action led him further into the trap.

Helen's mind also tricked her as her inner lusts were triggered by the circumstances, and she cried out her needs.

"Drink me! Oh, I'm so full I'm bursting! Drink me up!"

The lustful words triggered Longworthy's own reflexes, and he let his hand slide from its slippery refuge as his mouth moved downward from the tip of the saliva-wet breast, across the sleek belly and into the blonde forest below.

Helen's leg moved under his chest as she withdrew it from beneath him to lay it across his bask. Then his lips sought the swollen

rim of the flowing fountain, and his tongue caressed the fleshy petals as they opened still further to him. His hands reached upward to grasp the twin globes of her aching breasts, and she moaned constantly as her hips moved beneath his head.

Then a gigantic tremor shook her, and a rippling quiver travelled over her body as she found release.

But she could see under his chest and belly, and the extended shaft of his desire magnetized her.

Oh! I must have that! It's so swollen and loaded, and it was my body that made it that way! She twisted herself around and pulled her flooding fountain from Longworthy's lips, as she used elbows and hands and feet to reach under his arched body.

Her hand seized the firm, fleshy shaft and tentatively brought it down to her curious lips. As she ringed the purple-red tip with her mouth, her hand slipped back to caress the heavy bag behind it, then her other hand grasped the weapon at its base. She searched the entire circumference of the tip with her tongue, then thrust tenderly into the small orifice and wiggled gently. The throbbing of his pulse was communicated to her as it swelled in reflex.

Oh, spurt for me, Papa Longworthy! Give me yourself! She felt his fingers as they searched out her brimming pool and buried themselves in her hot flesh. Her hand squeezed caressingly at the hairy ball-sac it held, palpating the heavy testicles within, and she let the huge wand slide deeper into her, until the tip touched the rear of her palate. Her lust-filled mind was screaming her animal passions as she possessed the forbidden fruit of these male loins. Oh, Papa, I creamed so for you! My love flowered faster than you could drink it! Now pour your love into me!

Her thoughts seemed so loud to her, that she almost wondered why he couldn't hear them, too. Then something exploded in her head.

She felt the quivering tremor start to travel from where he was probing her wet nest, upward throughout her body. As her entire being shuddered in ecstasy, the hot, spurting streams in her mouth poured down to meet the other warmth. She swallowed and swallowed, and then everything went black.

When she came to her senses, she could hear the mocking sound of Fernández's laughter ringing in her ears. There were two unfamiliar odours in the atmosphere. One she guessed to be the chemical smell of the magnesium flare powder used to illuminate Consuelo's photographs. It took her a moment to identify the other. Then she brought up a tentative hand and moved it across her mouth. As she withdrew it, she opened her eyes, and watched as a long string of semen trailed from her chin to her finger.

Her eyes lifted to look past her sperm-drenched hand, and she met her father's gaze. With the return of his conscious mind to the sane control of his faculties, his eyes betrayed his sickness and misery with what they had done under the control of their subconscious lusts. She couldn't know just how much of his horror was due to her display of depravity, but at the thought of losing his love and respect, she was as heartsick as he possibly could be. The tears welled up in her eyes. "Oh, Papa Longworthy! I'm so ashamed!"

She thought that a little of the horror faded from his eyes, as his hand reached out to pat her consolingly. But when it touched the warm satin of her bare thigh, his hand jerked away Quickly, and he blushed with the memory of their more intimate bodily contacts.

"*Muy bien*," said Fernández. "This set of pictures will do very nicely. But we must make absolutely sure of our bargaining position, no? We now start the next act of our circus. You may use the bathroom. Consuelo!"

The blowzy girl took Helen's arm and led her out of the room and down the hall. In a few minutes, they returned, and Consuelo took Longworthy to the bathroom, a room that was mercifully blessed with modern plumbing: a water closet that flushed and a bidet. While they waited, Helen was turning over some frightening thoughts in her mind. What if the sponge and douche equipment had not been enough? What if she had *already* fallen pregnant with Osjami's child? She tried to drive from her mind the picture of the offspring he might give her – what would her smart Boston friends say if she gave birth to a... a *half-caste!* She shuddered, and as if he had guessed her thoughts the black man's grip on her arm tightened imperceptibly, and he led her over to the bed, where she sat down.

Longworthy returned, and Consuelo remained in the hall. Fernández studied Helen for a few seconds, and then looked at Longworthy.

"I think we will give you a rest, now, and bring our other performers up here. Consuelo, see to it that the girl has water with which to douche and so on." He nodded at Longworthy. "You – get your clothes on, and we will take you back below."

When they were dressed, they were escorted back downstairs to their shackles; it was the turn of her mother and brother now.

Osjami released Frank, and now the two of them were led upstairs. To Charlie

Longworthy's relief, like his daughter, Ruth was permitted to take her 'just-in-case' purse with her. It was very silent in the cellar for several minutes, and then Longworthy spoke to Helen.

"God knows what this will do to your mother. Sometimes I think she's stronger, mentally, than I am. But what they're going to do to her now may be more than she can take. God have mercy on me for getting us into this!"

Helen, whose mind was busy imagining the scenes that were about to take place upstairs, did not answer.

The silence returned to the dungeon like atmosphere. The light was off, now, and to Longworthy, it was as if he were a prisoner in some novel by Dumas. His ears strained to pick up any sounds from the rooms above them, but all he could hear was an occasional heavy sigh from Helen and the rasp of his own breathing.

Chapter 4

Ruth Longworthy had steeled herself to meet almost any kind of abuse she could imagine. What she had seen in the photos delivered to the hotel convinced her that she could expect sexual assaults from either Fernández, Osjami, or both. She had had no opportunity to learn what Charlie and Helen had undergone while upstairs.

She didn't really want to know. She could imagine all too easily the further rape of her golden young daughter by these Cubans. And she didn't like to think of that sleazy, smelly Consuelo toying with Charlie's equipment, either. She didn't like the thought of those family jewels, which had given her so many pleasurable delights, in the garbage-like vault of that Cuban whore!

Nor did she care to picture her son's defilement by the woman. Yet, she knew it must be intended. Just as she fully expected to be invaded by the Cubans who now ushered her into the bedroom.

"Take off all your clothing!" Fernández ordered them.

Ruth almost protested against their forcing both the mother and the son to disrobe in the same room. But she remembered the threats issued downstairs, and decided to hold her tongue. As she removed her clothes, she detected the faint smell of semen in the room. A little shudder ran through her. That smell was always an aphrodisiac trigger for her. Even now, under these awful circumstances, it got to her.

She felt their eyes on her, and knew they were admiring her ripe body, which had retained its lushness with scarcely an added wrinkle or ounce of fat, since Frank's birth. She was thinking of Frank, and of the delight she'd experienced when he nursed on her milk-laden breasts as an infant. Now, as he undressed in her presence with obvious embarrassment – she noticed that he was very much the virile young man. In recent years, since he'd struggled through the first stages of puberty, she hadn't seen him without at least a pair of shorts or bathing trunks. He certainly was not her "Little boy" any more. In fact, she coloured blushingly when he inadvertently looked her way.

She stood there, vulnerable in her nudity try, and felt the quick touch of his gaze on her body. It made her feel more exposed to be seen by her own son than by these depraved strangers who were their captors.

Frank was blushing, too. The sight of his mother's unclothed body affected him strangely. Mothers were supposed to be different from other women. He realized that they had the same basic equipment, but somehow it seemed indecent that this woman who had given birth to him and cared for him all these years, should have the ripe, exciting figure of a girl far younger than her thirty-five summers.

Those full, firm-looking orbs that he knew he had nursed as an infant showed almost no tendency to sag, and the sleek lines of her hips, swelling out from that tiny waist, were all too much like those photogravures of the latest pretty debutantes in one of the society magazines. He kept his eyes completely averted, after that one accidental glance, but the femaleness of that milky white body and the bright, golden bush which decorated the juncture of thighs and belly, remained as an image burned on his brain.

"Very well!" said Fernández, startling them both with the suddenness of his voice in the embarrassed silence of the room. "Get in the bed! Quickly!" Ruth moved slowly backward until her legs bumped the edge of the bed, then sat down.

"I am going to tell you what I told Mr. Longworthy. Then I shall expect complete cooperation from both of you: Mr. Longworthy has refused to pay us when his daughter's safety depended upon it. I am convinced that he will pay to protect the reputation of every member of his family. Pride can be a strange thing.

"Therefore, we will take pictures of all of you – pictures which he will be anxious to destroy, before they can be seen by others. If he then pays us what we ask, we will let him destroy the pictures. You see this is the only way we have of dealing with a man of his stubborn convictions.

"Now, we have wasted enough time with your family. So, from here on, you will do *exactemente* as you are told, quickly, and without hesitation. If you do not, there will be pain. Your daughter, Mrs. Longworthy, already bears a painful proof of what I tell you. It is up to you if you also receive much pain. So! We waste not another minute! Into bed, both of you!"

Ruth drew up her legs, keeping them chastely together, and lay out full length on the bed. Frank crawled in beside her, keeping to the other side of the bed. There were several inches of space between them.

"Now, you – Frank-ee, is it not? – you will place your left hand on her hip. Quickly!" Frank's hand reached out, and he had to turn his body toward her to stretch the distance. Ruth, out of the corners of her eyes, saw that he would have to slide his hand and wrist across the area of her womanly delta to obey the command, so she rolled over toward him on her side, moving the forbidden forest out of the danger zone. When his hand touched the warm flesh of her hip, she gasped involuntarily. The ends of his fingers were lightly resting on the sensitive skin of her buttock: a tingle went through her at the contact.

"Now, your mouth on her breast!" commanded Fernández.

Frank hesitated a fraction of a second, then saw the Cuban moving closer to Ruth's side of the bed. He was blowing on the tip of a lit small cigar, and there was an evil, joyful light in his eyes. Had Fernández been moving toward him, Frank was sure he would have refused to obey. But he knew it was his mother who would pay for it. And Fernández seemed to want an excuse to display his sadism.

Quickly, Frank moved closer, until his head was at the level of her breasts. He touched the side of the pale golden hillock with his lips, and Fernández stopped the advance of the glowing small cigar.

"Movement!" ordered Fernández. "Use your lips and tongue; stir up the nipple! We must have convincing photographs."

Frank's lips parted, and he traced a light trail up the side of the tender globe to the irregularly textured surface at its peak. He felt a thrill as the softness touched the tip of his tongue.

Ruth was struggling to control her illicit desires, but the warm damp lips and tongue were too much for her. She felt the blossoming of nipple as it rose between the caressing lips, and her lungs filled with a gasp of air that almost whistled through her teeth.

Frank felt the tender morsel spring into his mouth, and then the hidden memories of his infancy combined with the strong, urgent cravings of his virile young body, and he sucked at the springy titbit, then teased it with lips and tongue. The thrill of such a forbidden act struck him unexpectedly. His defences were not equal to the power of his cravings.

He worked hungrily at the tender meal, and the moaning of his mother's voice was a strange sound in his ears. Then her hands were grasping his head, moving him away from his exciting feast. He was panting as she guided his mouth to her other warm hemisphere, and the damp heat of his passionate exhalations stirred the nipple of this other globe to early blossom.

His lips seized it eagerly, and he sucked at its softness, stretching it from its first budding into a swollen sponge. Ruth moaned loudly as the action stirred her to the core.

"Take his *pinga* — hold it — grasp it with your fingers!" commanded the Cuban, and guessing correctly what he meant, Ruth reached under Frank's arm and sought the flesh of his manhood. As she reached, she had to roll slightly away from him with her hips, to make room for her exploring hand and arm, so that just as she grasped his rod, already stiff with excitement, the hand he had placed on her hip was trailed across the front of her upper thigh and then halted in the blonde forest of her loins.

She felt him swell in her hand as he thrilled to the feel of her heated flesh under his fingers. Then she whimpered as she spread her thighs, and the swelling outer lips of her womanhood parted, capturing his fingertips in the damp heat of her fleshy canyon.

Frank's pulse raced as he felt the hot lips under his fingers, and the wetness he encountered was an invitation to explore. His hand shifted as he sought out the uppermost cleft, then gently massaged the fleshy protrusion hidden there.

It was infinitely more exciting than previous experiences he'd had — most of them with the maids at home. This seemed so much more serious — so mature. Even as he felt the guilt of its wrongness, his passion increased. The hand which was closed over his pulsing hardness had started to move, and the friction was driving him wild.

"Now! Get above her, and put your cock inside her!" came the order.

He tried to move, but his knees were like jelly, and it took him quite a while to get up on all fours and position himself above her. Ruth had started to spread her legs wider in anticipation, but suddenly she rebelled. A belated surge of conscience made her close her thighs to her son as he hovered above her. Then the pain struck!

Fernández's lighted small cigar pressed against her neck, and he ground it against the tender flesh. She shrieked as the pain spread over her face, the tears rolled down onto the bed in streams. Frank started to clamber up out of his position, ready to attack the sadist in anger. His stiffened member lost its rigidity, and his excitement cooled as if he'd been thrust into a tub of ice water.

The Cuban watched him start to spring from the bed, then cut short any ideas about revenge.

"You will not help your mother by being troublesome. *Al contrario!* Every move you make against us everything you do to delay our little circus will cost her another painful burn. You do not want that beautiful face destroyed, do you?"

Frank settled back onto the bed, defeated. He was half-kneeling, half-squatting, and his eyes were dark with his frustrated ed anger. But Fernández laughed at him, then spoke to Ruth.

"The same is true with you. You have felt the taste of my displeasure. After this, when it is you who fails to cooperate, your son will suffer the pain. Now! You will both begin once more! At the point where you stopped! Quickly!"

Frank looked down at himself, and both Ruth and the Cuban followed his gaze. It was obvious that he was in no condition to penetrate anything. Ruth's heart went out to him. Even his virile father had suffered temporary impotency when lesser disturbances had interrupted his boudoir athletics. But Fernández was laughing at him.

"We will fix that. Consuelo! See if you can't wake up the young man's sleeping beauty with your clever mouth!" The slattern moved toward the bed, running a pink tongue around her grinning lips in an obscene parody of sexual gluttony.

"No!" Ruth shouted. "I won't have her touch him! If it must be done, I will do it myself!" As Consuelo stopped in her tracks, and the satanic Cuban grinned his enjoyment of the maneuver, Ruth reversed her position hurriedly, crawling toward the foot of the bed where her son still remained in his squatting-kneeling position.

She placed a hand on his thigh as she neared her goal, and gave it a loving squeeze. She spoke to him in a low voice, not looking up at his face, as if trying to avoid any further emotional pressures.

"Close your eyes, and think of nothing but the moment. Try to let your body function as it will, and enjoy what has to happen. It is the only way we will prevent further misery."

With no more hesitation than it took to get out the few words, she bent over him. As her lips touched him, high up on his inner thigh, he felt a thrilling tingle of contact. Then her tongue was snaking out, trailing up across the curly thatch of his groin, then down to the base of his limp penis.

She took the flaccid shaft in her mouth, right at the base of its connection to his torso, raking it gently with her teeth. She softly shook her head, worrying the reluctant warrior in her mouth. Then her teeth relaxed their grip, and she slid her lips and tongue out toward the tip, astonished by the growing length of her son's awakening member.

He's just like his father, she thought. Every inch a man, and plenty of inches! Even when he's not ready for action! It feels so good in my mouth. Even Charlie doesn't know how much I really like to have his big cock in my mouth! He'd probably be shocked. I believe he thinks that I do this for him just to please him, but I can get creamed over the feel and taste of his cock quicker than any other way. I love it when he fucks me with it, but it's so much more exciting to have that hot, soft-hard flesh in my mouth! Oh, Charlie! Your cock excites me so!

As she gradually managed, by association, to convince herself that it was her mate, and not her son, whose stiffening flesh she was having with her lips and tongue, she felt her legs being moved by Frank's firm, young hands. What a wonderful mother! Frank was thinking. To keep me from being contaminated by that filthy, syphilitic whore, she's taking my cock in her sweet mouth. And, God help me! I love it. It's driving me wild! I've got to do it for her, too, to help her try to get some relief from this, and keep her from worrying about what we're being forced to do.

With this admittedly shaky logic uppermost in his mind, he grasped her kneeling legs, and moved them out from under her, almost making her lose her oral grasp on him. Then he rolled her over, changing his position until he was poised with his mouth over her blonde-feathered loins. He moved her thighs apart, and watched as her fleshy nether lips – swollen from the blood they had engorged during the earlier excitement – parted to reveal the delightful, glistening pinkness of

her most private area.

The faint, pissy muskiness of her rose to his nostrils, and he was surprised to find that the scent excited him. He touched his tongue to the swollen lips, stroking them as they darkened with the in creasing re-engorgement of blood. Now they were beginning to become even more wet, and the lubricious flow of her passion seemed to replace the moisture as fast as he could lick it up.

She was making little, whimpering, mewing sounds from around the swollen shaft of flesh that filled her mouth, and her breath, which had to come from her nostrils while her mouth was filled, felt hot on Frank's hairy sac, which lay on her face. It aroused him to new levels of excitement, and he feasted hungrily but tenderly on the wet, magenta flesh of her opened blossom.

Her hips were rotating slowly beneath his head, with an occasional gentle thrust upward, making his tongue and lips press frequently at the erectly swollen bud of her clitoris. He grasped the fleshy protrusion with his lips, revelling in its unbelievable soft surface and tender hardness from within. His nose was dipping into the wet, flowing entrance of her passage.

Who would have thought a woman's cunt would be so delicious! he marvelled. It's so damned excitingly female, open like that, and helpless. I can plunder it all I want. He was lost in the depth of his passionate experience, and the body he assaulted so eagerly was now just another exciting female body.

Ruth's juices were so stirred up – first by her oral excitement, then by the thoroughness of the attentions being given her heated nether flesh – that she was lost in the deep twilight that precedes a woman's complete fulfilment.

Finally, her flowing loins were so swollen with her driving pulse that she let the huge penis slip from her lips as it pulled back in one of the pumping strokes which had been thrusting into her mouth, and cried out in her aching passion.

"Drink me! Oh-h-h! Drink me all up! Devour me! Oh-h-h!"

The mouth worked faster, trying to remove the lubricious cream of her overflow as fast as it could appear. The excitement was too much for him, and his penis – now rubbing against the lips and chin below it, started to leak its first drops from the safety valve.

Ruth felt the first hot drops spatter on her neck and breasts, and she grabbed the pulsing shaft and forced it back into her mouth. As it pumped its spurting gobs of semen, she swallowed it, and continued to suck and swallow, while milking the rear of the long rod with the hand that grasped it.

Frank was moaning into the hot, musky wetness of the blossom on which he feasted, until he felt as though his very soul was being sucked from his body. Then he gave a loud groan, and rolled from his position, flopping exhausted, facedown onto the bed.

Ruth, on reaching the second of her complete orgasms, lay there as spent as Frank. She felt Frank's hand gently pat her thigh, and realized that it was not the aftermath love pat of a satisfied male, so much as a consoling gesture from son to mother. She was also aware of the final shutter click as Consuelo filmed the evidence of their collapse.

She realized that her legs were wide open, and her wet nest felt cool in the slight breeze which had begun to flow in through the bedroom window. She wondered vaguely if this were the beginning of one of the tropical storms her husband had described.

"Very well. Now you may use the bathroom. You first, *Señora* Longworthy."

When she had swept away all the excess water she could – there were no towels in evidence – she turned to the open door where Consuelo had stood, observing her and waiting to take her down the hall back to the bedroom.

Back in the room, Consuelo motioned with

her head to Frank, and he followed her to the bathroom. He entered the room and tried to shut the door, but Consuelo prevented him, waving the small pistol at his belly.

"I am to keep you under watch at all times."

She laughed.

"Certainly a handsome man like you need not be ashamed to be seen by a woman. You should be proud of that beautiful thing you wear between your legs. I think I will ask Fernández if I can have some of it."

He blushed, but stood there, trying to relieve his bladder as she watched. He found that he had to concentrate, but finally his desperate physical need overcame his psychological block, and he urinated a heavy stream into the porcelain water closet.

Consuelo watched as he shook off the last drops, then – as he turned to look for the basin to wash his hands – she lifted her skirt with her free hand, keeping the pistol trained on him. As she grabbed it up past her thighs and held it bunched against her belly, he saw the black hair of her pubic mound and the slightly distended outer lips, a wet gleam of dark red flesh. As he watched, the lips seemed to wink at him, and Consuelo chuckled lustily.

"See what a nice kiss it makes for you?" she asked. "Would it not be nice to have it kiss like that on the end of your so beautiful *pinga*?" She continued to laugh as he washed his hands and shook them to dry them, then shepherded him back to the others.

"Well. The hero of our little drama is back. Now we can proceed." Fernández was relishing every moment of his domination over them.

"You did not yet complete the orders I gave you. It seems that you were both so hungry for soixante-neuf that you could not stop to do a little fucking for the camera. *Muy Bien!* You have just reversed the order in which we had planned to photograph you. Now, we will continue with the other: this will not be difficult for you, I feel certain..."

With a lewd smirk, he gestured them toward the bed, and they crawled onto the crumpled bedclothes and lay there, waiting to see what was next.

"Madame, you have expended the young man's seed with your hunger. Now you will make love to him a little, until he is ready to penetrate you, and then you will take him inside you for our final pictures." As he finished speaking, Fernández blew warningly on the glowing tip of a freshly lit small cigar. Ruth turned to her son, reaching out to him, and his arms opened to take her. There was fear and guilt and shame in their eyes as their gazes met briefly. But there was something else. This first opportunity to look into each other's eyes told them both that they were sharing pleasure as well as pain and fear.

They embraced each other with a powerful need. The need to drive away the feelings of guilt and shame, and to drown themselves in the forced pleasure of their contact Neither knew what the future held for them, after these forbidden activities, but they knew that the quickest way to end things was to resolve the problem at hand – meet the requirements of the sadistic Fernández.

Their lips met, and for the first time in his life, Frank was not thinking like a son when he kissed his mother's lips. And Ruth could only compare it in reverse, as she recalled the time when – at fourteen, and full of the bursting forces of her blossoming womanhood – she had kissed her father on the mouth, and knew that she must never kiss him again, excepting on the cheek.

Now, her memory of that journey into puberty seemed to stimulate her quiescent sexuality into fresh stirrings that trembled through her rapidly heating body. She thrust her tongue into Frank's mouth, and he eagerly sucked at it, and caressed it with his own tongue. In seconds, she felt the stiffening evidence of his youthful virility rising steadily, its firm tip tracing a path up her thighs until it pressed against the flesh of her soft lower belly.

His hands were caressing her body,

now. His fingers traced pencils of heat over her back and hips. Then he was clutching the firm cheeks of her buttocks, massaging them tenderly to the tempo of his increasing passion.

She moved her hips until his hardened flesh pressed her just where she wanted it, then made tiny movements which kept up a constant massage of her needy spot.

They were gasping for air, now, and their mouths separated. He moved his head, kissing her on neck and shoulders, then trying to kiss the swollen tips of her breasts. The shift of his body removed the source of her greatest pleasure, but she waited, giving him his feast at both breasts until the nipples were achingly distended, and she was moaning from the results.

Then she pulled his head up to hers, and kissed him again. As his head moved, his torso shifted, and the hot head of his stiff tool was pulsing against her belly. She opened her thighs, and slipped her hips upward, then let them ride back downward with his captive wand, sandwiched between the slick labia that had grasped it.

Once again, she started to move in short, gentle strokes, causing the captured flesh to massage her own tiny wand. Their mouths were tightly pressed together, their tongues thrusting and searching.

As the momentum of her passion gained speed, she suddenly sucked his tongue deep into her mouth, and his hands slid upward to cup the firm globes of her breasts. Her hands went down to grasp him, then she guided him into the spread petals of her wet, open passage.

Then he was inside her, and plunging deeply into the grasping folds that seemed to urge him on, faster and faster. Until he felt the fluttering touch of some wildly moving thing inside her, nibbling delicately at the sensitive head of his penis

My beautiful mother, he thought, from some subconscious area that refused to trigger his passion-dulled conscience. I'm fucking my own sweet, juicy mother! Oh, God! What's that inside her that's grabbing my cock like that? I've got to get away from it. It's driving me out of my mind!

He pulled backward to escape the maddening teasing of her involuntarily grazing hold on him. Then he was thrusting, pumping, in and out, as she rotated her buttocks beneath him. Then she cried out in the throes of her heated excitement.

"Oh yes! Fuck me hard! Stick it in all the way! *Oh-h-h-h-h!*" She writhed under him, and her mouth was tight, teeth close together, lips barely parted. A hissing sound came from between her teeth as she fought for air, while her jaw was tensed in ecstasy.

Then she was trembling, and her body shook under him with the depth of her climax. He had just probed to her innermost wall, and the tiny hand-like grasping had him again! He felt the fluttering over his sensitive nerve ends, then he lost control, and his hot fluid poured into the fleshy folds of her pussy. He groaned as the ecstatic feeling overwhelmed him, and then he lay still, poised above her, weight resting on hands and knees, until he could stop shaking enough to roll off to the side.

He came inside her. For a moment, he was horrified, remembering what he'd heard of the monstrous offspring that could result from such inbreeding. My God! I shot my load into my mother! Oh, God! I hope the equipment of which she spoke works! Oh, my own poor, darling mother!

"You may use the bathroom now," said Fernández. Frank was glad he could wait until his mother was through. He felt as if his bones had turned to rubber. Consuelo was coating the surfaces of her last few photographic prints with the preservative which fixed them permanently, so Fernández guarded Ruth as she went down the hall. She waited for him to leave the room, but he stood there, grinning at her.

She sighed in resignation as she moved

over the bidet and squatted down to straddle it. She busied herself with the taps and flushed out the blobs and strings of whitish semen her son had spurted into her. Then she cleansed her entire genital area with the soothing water.

When she turned her head to see if Fernández was watching her, she sucked in her breath as her lips met the tip of the Cuban's rigid cock. He had stealthily moved up beside her as she sat there, washing herself, and had levered his member out of his slacks, holding it right beside her cheek.

As her lips opened to gasp, he was ready, and the hard flesh went into her mouth so far that his hairy belly, which peeped through the open slot of his underpants, pressed against her nose. His hands were around her head, and he began pumping himself into her mouth and throat, until she started to gag.

Then he withdrew it a little, and she grabbed the rear part of the fleshy shaft to keep it from again going in so deeply. She was wise enough not to resist his attentions, and began to work on him, trying to finish the matter as quickly as possible.

But the treacherous spirit of her own sexuality betrayed her, and soon she found herself hungrily mouthing him and stroking his shaft with one hand, while her other hand slipped into his shorts and kneaded his sperm-bloated balls with gentle, but eager caresses.

He was groaning at the sensations she induced in him, and soon he dug his fingers in her blonde tresses and cried out, as he worked his hips viciously to drive his meat into this elegant woman's mouth.

Suddenly he was spewing his lust inside her, and it flowed down her throat as she sucked the swollen tip so expertly that he groaned and withdrew it. One last trickle was just seeping out, and it made a sticky string that drooled across her lips and chin, then hung wetly, dangling over her breasts.

She leaned over the basin and filled it with water, then rinsed off her face breasts and then stood up. Fernández was smiling as he tucked himself back into his clothes. Then he waited as she poured some more water into a glass, gargled with it, and spat it out. He laughed at her.

"It would seem that the juice of the Cuban is not as tasty as that of the American," he said. "But then perhaps it is only that you are accustomed to the one taste more than the other." He laughed again at his own joke as they went back down the hall.

Ruth dressed while Frank was in the bathroom. When he had returned and dressed, they were led out the stairway, and taken back into the cellar.

Helen was looking anxiously at them as

they were brought in, but Longworthy, from years of habit, was sleeping after his sexual episode. As soon as the mother and son were shackled, Fernández and Consuelo came over and unlocked her cuffs. Then they unlocked Longworthy's, after which they shook him until he was awake.

"We will now finish our photographic portraits of you two," he said. Then perhaps we can all get some sleep, no?"

Chapter 5

It was deathly quiet in the cellar after Longworthy and Helen were taken away for the second time. Frank could hear his mother breathing in long, sighing breaths, and he thought he could hear the pounding of his own heart. But all else was quiet. He thought about what he had just been through – really, what his mother had been forced to endure.

Like most well-brought-up young men, he idolized his beautiful mother, and he found it impossible to believe that she had been involved in the fantastic sequence of events he had just left upstairs. It just couldn't be! And now, Helen and their father were back up there, being forced into still more shameful acts. When would it end? Would they really be allowed to leave if the ransom were paid?

Then his mind shifted again, and he was trying to assess his feelings during the recent episode. I knew it was my mother there with me! And yet I enjoyed it! I really wanted to taste her body in my mouth – I loved the smell of her sex – the taste of her juices – the feel of her heat pouring out of her body at me. My God! What kind of madman am I, anyhow? I even loved it when I was fucking her! The feel of her juicy cunt wrapped around me was like nothing I've ever felt before. And what was that inside her that seemed to grip and squeeze my cock? My God! Is there something wrong with her, too? Could I really have seemed like a lover to her, or something?

He was working himself up to a nervous panic that he had never known before. The perspiration was gathered on his brow and upper lip. He hadn't realized it, but he was panting with the effort of thinking and searching in the recesses of his mind for some answers. In short, he was frightened with the immensity of what he knew had been a very terribly wrong thing. A thing in which he'd been forced to participate, but which he had actually enjoyed, once he'd started!

It was several minutes after his teeth started chattering with his nervousness, and with the cold of the dank cellar, which chilled him as his perspiration dried, that his mother spoke to him. "Frank! What's the matter? Are you ill?"

He was silent, except for his gasping and chattering Then he bubbled over. All of his fears and guilts and shame – all the things that were threatening his sanity – he poured out to her. After all, for the greater part of his young life he'd turned to her whenever he couldn't solve his own problems. He thought he'd outgrown his need of her as a confessor and comforter. But he could never have foreseen such events as this.

Ruth heard him out. At times he was almost incoherent in his eagerness to get everything off his chest, hoping that complete confession would relieve him of his aching, bursting burden. But she understood him all too well everything he said. When he finally finished, running down like a record on a phonograph that needed another winding up to get it up to normal speed, it was again silent in the old cellar. She thought a long time before she spoke. She had to be sure that she said the right thing. This could affect him for the rest of his life!

"Frank, I may be able to answer you on everything, and I may not. I'll try to do my best. You know that I love you very much, and that I'll always love you. You know that, don't you?" She waited until he pulled himself together sufficiently to answer.

"Of course. I've never doubted that!" he replied.

"Just keep that in the back of your mind, then, no matter what else we discuss. Will you – can you do that?"

"Yes. And mother? ... no matter what else

I said … I'll always love you just as I have since I could remember."

"I know, Frank. I knew that the moment you turned to me to help you with all this that's bothering you so much." She almost choked up on her emotions, then got a grip on herself, and continued.

"Frank, I'll have to talk to you darned plainly. I know that your father, thank God, has brought you up with all the basic sexual knowledge you need, but this mess we're in now is something no one could be expected to foresee.

"You've taken enough of the basic elements of human psychology to understand how closely we parallel the lower animals in certain of our normal functions. What always seems so hard to understand is that the entire package we call civilization – all the things we try to instil in ourselves, educate ourselves with, as it were really is only a very thin coating which we manage to keep pulled over the more basic, more deeply ingrained things inside us.

"Of course, everyone is an individual, because he has his own very special formula, which combines the things he has inherited, the things he has learned, and the environment in which he is brought up. There are other factors, too, but these affect us most.

"Now, you won't find two men much

farther apart as individuals than your father and that Fernández." She used the Cuban's name as if it were the filthiest thing she could utter.

"Charlie is a big, husky, he-man type, who pretends that he doesn't have a good education sometimes, especially when he's with those who really haven't. He talks as if he'd just as soon beat you as look at you, sometimes. But you know as well as I do – almost as well, anyhow – that he's really an old softy, and more gentleman than anything else.

"Fernández, on the other hand, pretends to be a gentleman, uses flowery speech to cover his crude thoughts and drives. He pretends to be so very refined in all other ways, yet you know – when he tells you he'll do something very horrible that he means it, for there seems to be nothing too foul or brutal for his mind to dream up or his conscience to object to. And yet, if those two were facing each other in anything like an equal battle, I'd bet on your father. Because underneath all of the veneer that we see his personality that we know, his many fine characteristics – lies that basic that we do not know. I think he might very well break the Cuban in little pieces.

"Something like that can take place in any of us. No matter what we are like all the rest of our lives, underneath we are, after all, very basic creatures. Some of us have as many surprising differences in our basic nature as we do in the side of us which we show to the world everyday.

"Now, your father and I are both individuals who love our bodily pleasures. And I'm afraid that both you and Helen have inherited more than your share of this propensity. I can only say that I am not surprised you are so much like your father. And Helen is probably much more like me than I have wanted to believe.

"When we were forced into a situation such as this, Frank, it was inevitable that we burst out of our civilized wrappers and exposed the depth of our sexualities. We were at those moments just two human individuals who were unfortunate enough to be placed in that very set of conditions.

"Sure, we could blame ourselves for breaking down, for giving in to our baser natures. But what would it buy us? It's happened. We couldn't undo it if we spent the rest of our lives and all of our family's resources. So, the only thing to do is to try to shove it into the back of our minds as far as it will go. If we find that we have trouble living with it, we'll just have to bring it out and discuss it again. But I hope we can think of it as a very unfortunate but irrevocable part of our lives that we need not think of, again.

"Before we do try to forget it, dear one, it might be well to get the last bit of value out of it. Let me tell you that if you ever have one of those moments when you doubt yourself as a man, for any reason, you can remember that your mother gave you top honours.

"You're every bit the man your father is in all ways. You're thoughtful, gentle, and very exciting to a woman. The girl who gets you for keeps – and any others in the meantime will be very lucky. I'll always be proud that you're my son, Frank."

She was silent, and the cellar was full of her presence as it had not been all the time she spoke. Frank felt the magnetism of this wonderful woman who was his mother, and almost – not quite, but almost – he was glad that they had shared the rigours of this day. It was a lot of female, and a lot of heart that he had the good fortune to call mother. He wept quietly, unashamedly, for a while. Then he spoke his gratitude.

"You're great, Mother! I've known that for a long time, but after today, I'm afraid that you're some kind of impossible combination of saint and sweetheart that just might have spoiled me for all the other women in the world. I only hope that I'm lucky enough to get one just a little bit like you."

"Thank you, Frank." She stopped for a moment, then thought of something else. "It's a hell of a way for it to happen, but I don't think we've ever been so close as right now. We've shared the very worst moments of our lives together, and yet found joy in them. Not many people can say that."

Chapter 6

"*No hay suficiente luz para hacer la foto, espera,*" protested Consuelo.

"What did she say?" Longworthy asked his daughter. His Spanish had been limited, in the old days, to slowly spoken phrases of simple vocabularies. Now he remembered very little of that.

"She says the lighting isn't good enough for taking pictures, now. I think they must have run out of the magnesium." Helen hoped that this meant a reprieve. If further photography was postponed until morning, maybe they could find some way to escape in the night.

"We will use the parlour," decided Fernández, dashing Helen's hopes for a delay. They were herded out of the bedroom, which they had just entered before Consuelo's protest, and soon found themselves in a fairly large living room. The wall-to-wall carpeting was old but good, and there were a few pieces of furniture scattered around, none of which seemed to belong.

On the walls were a number of mirrors,

which seemed to be built into the structure, or cleverly affixed to seem very permanent. In several places, the faint outlines of rectangular shapes revealed where pictures had been hung.

The place gave the appearance of a house deserted by its former occupants, then commandeered by Fernández and company as a temporary headquarters. Helen wondered where the furniture had been obtained, guessing that it might well have been stolen from other homes in the area.

Longworthy paid little attention to the details of the room. He was just barely awake, and beginning to feel again the resentments and discouragements which had bothered him since his capture, as well as the guilt and shame he had experienced after the previous episode with his daughter.

"Here, on the sofa," commanded Fernández. They moved toward the huge sofa, the back of which folded over and down to create a fair-sized bed.

"The clothes – quickly! " he ordered, and the father and daughter sullenly removed their clothes again. This time they piled them on a long low table nearby.

Consuelo had opened the drapes that covered glass-panelled doors leading onto a terrace. A poorly tended garden could be seen. It was on the side away from the track, and the shrubbery hid the doorway from outsiders.

The light that entered the room seemed to be magnified by the several mirrors, and it was considerably brighter than the bedroom.

"Let me see; I think *Señor* Longworthy will sit on the edge of the bed ..." Longworthy obliged. "... And the *Señorita* will sit on his lap to begin." Helen obediently seated herself across her father's legs. She could feel the warmth of him against her thighs, and the fine covering of hair tingled where it touched her skin.

"No. Not like that. Turn and face him, with a leg on either side of him." Fernández was playing by ear, as if he were a directive genius setting up a scene for a silent movie camera.

Helen lifted a leg and swung it over and around, past Longworthy's head. He couldn't help but see the pink flash of her spread vulva as her thighs separated so widely. That, and the way her one breast bounced briefly after her knee had struck it during the move, returned him to the illicitly excited plateau he had reached earlier.

Helen, who had grasped her father by the shoulders to make the shift, leaning back on his lap to clear his head with her leg, had caught a glimpse of me soft, white penis which she had coveted until today, and which she had possessed with her mouth less than two hours ago. It made the same little thrills run through her now, no matter how she had intended to control her reactions this time.

While they had been in the cellar alone, she tried twice to talk to him, hoping they could help each other in some way. She felt that if she must continue to carry the burden of her incestuous enjoyment all alone, she would crack up. But Longworthy had slept soundly, and she hadn't had the heart to make more than a token attempt to wake him with her quiet words. Now, she was even more tense than before, like a tightly-wound spring.

As she settled into the new pose Charlie Longworthy automatically put his hands on her hips, helping her to balance on his lap. The contact doubled the sensations that travelled between them with Helen's hands on his shoulders. "Let us have some kissing, now," said Fernández.

As if hypnotized, they moved their heads together. In the beginning it was a zombie-like manoeuvre, as they reacted to the command, knowing the penalties for hesitation. But as their lips met, both of them knew the defeat of their individual resolutions.

The damp warmth of their bodies conducted each tiny tic and movement of every muscle. Even the slight tensions caused by trying to stay balanced in their positions as they moved to kiss, were amplified into caresses and significant movements, as the animal lusts within each body interpreted the small contacts and responded in kind.

Helen's moist lips parted, and she felt the hot tongue enter between them and caress the inner sides of her lips. As she sucked at the intruder hungrily, she felt the hard pressure of Longworthy's stiffening member as it rose under her, slapping meatily against the tender sensitivities of her anus.

Her buttocks squeezed together in reflex, and they trapped the head of the hard instrument between them. This further excited the man, and he reacted by a muscular contraction, which made the rod pulse into life, increasing its size and hardness.

It was a vicious circle. The feel of the swelling penis between her cheeks stirred Helen's inner juices, and they began to seep from the parted outer lips of her fleshy blossom, warming and dampening the base of her father's penis.

Something like a low growl emanated from Longworthy's lips as he tore them from hers, and then trailed a fiery thrill down her neck to the peak of a breast. Her nipple stiffened into a rigid erection which popped into his mouth, and he sucked at it thirstily, as though it could provide him with milk.

Helen's fleshy slit was leaking her juices all over his thighs as she writhed under the treatment. Then she tilted her hips and pulled back to release the rigid prisoner from her buttocks, letting it slip forward to dip into the slippery trough of her passion.

As it slid upward, between the swollen petals, gathering juices as it moved, it became trapped where the upper extremes of the lips were joined, and pressed tightly against the fleshy nubbin of her clitoris. She gave a little squeal of joy, and rubbed herself against the newcomer with little wriggling movements.

Longworthy's mouth switched to her other breast, and it bloomed under his kiss, eager to be taken and sucked. Then Helen whimpered her weakening defences as the massage between her legs made her tense and relax with exquisite, unbearable pleasure. She arched her back and pressed harder against him, then shuddered a giant tremor, moaning as it shook her. When she relaxed, Longworthy felt her wet heat leave him briefly then her hand reached down and grasped him tucking the achingly engorged head of his member into her hungry flesh.

As he felt himself slip within the inner lips which encircled her passage, his head was pulled from her breast, and drawn back up to place their mouths together again.

The tender, wrinkled folds of her passage

seemed to suck him within her depths, and he thought he could feel every part of that pulsating passage as it worked at him, drawing him farther inside. She vacuumed his tongue deep into her mouth.

I'm swallowing him at both ends, she thought, exulting at the sense of possession it gave her. His sweet tongue in my mouth, and his wonderful cock in my hungry cunt! I don't care what happens after this – Papa Longworthy is filling me from head to pussy, and it feels so good I hope I die before it stops!

Longworthy was less fortunate – or unfortunate, as the case might be. He was experiencing the miserable coincidence of having his lusts and his conscious mind fully awakened at the same time. As he felt the hungers of his strongly sexual nature seize him and take control, he began to realize what was taking place, even more vividly than he had at the earlier session in the bedroom.

A creature of habit, Longworthy had been used to using the period right after waking in the mornings, to lie and think about the recent successes and failures in his business involvements, and to plan the strategy for the day or days to come.

His mind, now fully awake after the sleep in the cellar, began to appreciate the ghastliness of his present predicament all too

well. It was bad enough to be forced into this, but to be unable to close off the conscious mind, to be forced to think on it – concentrate on it mercilessly as it took place – that was agony. Especially when it was so damnably enjoyable!

Lord! She's enjoying this as much as her mother does! The little minx is literally eating me up! And I love it, God help me! That little cunt of hers is so juicy and hot and squirmy, and it grabs at me as if it were starved! What in the name of God is going to happen to us? Our family is being turned into a bunch of perverted beasts!

Helen could hear her father groaning, but she took it for the sounds of his lustful enjoyment of her. Unaware of the agonising conflict he was enduring, she gloried in the way she was exciting him to moan. It stirred her to even greater passion, and her lubricant was literally streaming from her hyper-stimulated glands.

"Fuck me hard! Oh-h-h-h! Fuck it into me! Dig it way up inside me!" Her words were growled out as she lifted her mouth from his to beg him for more. "Oh-h-h! Fill my whole... *cunt* with it! Oh-h-h! God! You are fetching me! Don't let me go empty! Squirt me full! Oh-h-h-h!"

She panted and gasped as she bucked around on his lap like a wildcat.

"Oh! *Papa!* Fill me or I shall die! I can't stand it all hungry and empty like this! Oh-oh-oh-*ohhhh!* I am spending... *ohhhh!*" She stiffened as she reached her peak and began to topple. Then she felt the pumping of his pulsing fluids as they splashed against her innermost walls.

"Oh Lord! I'm spending too... inside you, my girl!" Longworthy moaned as he loosed himself. Then he was holding her tightly, pulling her soft buttocks to him, pouring himself into her in molten jets, thrusting as deeply as he could, even as he hated himself for it.

He toppled over backward on the bed, taking her with him. They lay there, breathing heavily, still locked together, until Longworthy felt a strange sensation, as though he were being tickled at the base of his now overly sensitized penis. Then his balls were being wetly tickled. He knew that Helen's hands were both on his neck. What could be happening? He looked downward past the creamy body that lay on top of him. A mass of flying black hair was moving around at the edge of the bed. Then he looked up to the mirror just opposite the sofa on a nearby wall, and he could see what was taking place.

That damned Consuelo! She's licking my cock and balls, and mouthing around Helen's little cunt as if she were starving! My God!

What a bunch of perverts and sadists! I've must get us out of here!

He moved to separate them, wanting to halt the prostitute's unclean intrusion into the episode. From seeing and smelling her, he didn't want any part of her touching him or his. But as he felt his limp member pull out of the snug sheath of his daughter's vagina, the sucking sound it made was followed by another, similar sound.

God! She's sucked me into her mouth! He tried to pull away from the feasting harpy, but Helen's weight on top of him kept him from freeing himself. And Consuelo had both of Helen's legs in her hands, one of them very high up. As Helen's hips began to gyrate, he realized where that hand really was!

"Fernández!" he called out. "We've done what you told us to do-you have your pictures – now let us out of here. What that woman is doing has nothing to do with your pictures!"

"*Señor* Longworthy! You would not begrudge the photographer a small bonus, would you? She has had to watch very much and it makes her very excited. Relax and allow her a little pleasure. Then you can clean up and put on your clothes."

Longworthy's head sank back on the bed, and he heaved a sigh of resignation. He felt his member stiffening in spite of his revulsion, as the girl expertly tongued its tingling surfaces. Then it was rock-hard again, and she was sucking and milking it with her mouth, while working her hand in the depths of Helen's hot, sperm-flooded cunt. Helen was moving wildly on top of her father as the trained fingers delved into her with merciless precision.

Then Helen's head moved over her father, and her mouth found his. She tongued his lips until they opened, and plunged her tongue between them into his mouth. The feel of her warm breasts on his chest, and the going-over Consuelo was giving him, loosed his animal instincts once more.

He brought his own tongue into locked combat with Helen's, and then he was sucking her tongue into his mouth, famished again for the sweet nectar of her youthful juices. She was wiggling in her excitement as Consuelo worked at the centre of her passion, and began to moan into her father's mouth as she neared her goal.

Then he felt himself opening up. As Consuelo took more and more of him into her mouth, Helen took back her tongue, and then sucked Longworthy's up into her mouth with a surprising strength. He felt his insides explode.

Helen bunched up in a writhing bundle as she screamed out her release, and her hot, wet feathery flesh came down on his belly, accompanied by Consuelo's sloppy wet hand, and he was draining out of the tip of his member, as if the Cuban girl were stealing his soul. He moaned at the awful totality of his orgasm; it seemed as if it would never stop. Then he felt her mouth leave his organ with a final, milking tug, heard her swallow repeatedly.

Helen, sighing faintly, rolled off him and lay beside him on the bed. Both were replete. It was almost as if their insides had been turned inside out.

Longworthy looked up to see Consuelo regaining her feet. She lifted her filthy skirt with a shiny-wet hand and wiped her juice-drenched face and chin. As she dried her face, her free hand massaged her black-haired pubic mound, parting the thickened lips until her dripping pinkness gleamed wetly at the observers.

"You can go to the bathroom, now," conceded Fernández.

"But I am not finish with them!" Consuelo protested, rubbing her swollen nether lips with one hand, and her upper lip and nose with the other.

"Go see Osjami, then. I want these people to rest. Tomorrow, *Señor* Longworthy goes for the money, *no es verdad?*"

Helen had pulled herself together and started for the bathroom. Fernández followed her out of the room. Consuelo pouted sullenly, watching Longworthy as he sat up on the edge of the sofa bed. She walked over to him and thrust her hips out.

"Be nice to me. Give me some pleasure. You will not be sorry!" She reached out and picked up his hand, trying to place it in the wet nest of her excitement. He jerked it away from her grasp with a curse.

"You filthy, stinking whore! I wouldn't touch your diseased cunt for anything! You're lower than the dirtiest animal. You're even worse than Fernández. At least he tries to look clean!" His anger boiled up at the disgusting uncleanliness of her.

Fernández and Helen came back into the room, and the girl started to dress as Longworthy got to his feet and headed for the bathroom. As he went into the hall, he heard Consuelo yell after him.

"I will make you sorry, rich American! *No one* can talk like that to Consuelo!" She lapsed into Spanish, rattling it off at Fernández, who had followed Longworthy into the hall. He cut her off with a few words, and then accompanied the millionaire to the bathroom.

When the victims had been led back to the cellar and shackled, and the family was again left to themselves, Longworthy asked his daughter what the conversation was about. She was quiet for a minute, and then answered him in a low voice, so that the other two could not hear.

"She was very angry with you for scorning her and calling her names. To get even she asked Fernández to give her Frank to play with."

"What did he say?" Longworthy felt a chill travel up his back.

"He told her that he'd see – after you left to get the money!"

"Damn him to hell! He can't do that! It's not part of the bargain. We did everything they ordered and they have the pictures. Now I have to get the money, or even if they release us those pictures could turn up anywhere to haunt us. Lord! What a horrible mess!"

"Actually, Papa Longworthy, he can do anything he wants. Until all of us are free, he has all the winning cards! You'd better talk to him and try to reason with him about Frank. It wouldn't do to make him mad. He thinks you've caused him enough trouble by refusing to pay the ransom in the first place."

Longworthy studied his daughter's face, and then took a quick look at Ruth and Frank. Both had their eyes closed. He turned back to Helen.

"You think so, too, don't you? You think I should have paid when you first turned up missing, don't you?" His voice was bitter. Helen couldn't be sure whether the bitterness was directed at himself or at her. He could have come to the decision that he'd been wrong in his lifelong opinions about ransoming. Or he could just suspect that she blamed him for all they'd been put through.

"You did what you thought was right, Papa. No one could ask you to act against the things you believe in. As I told you before, I'm proud that you had the courage of your convictions when it came to a real test. I know it wasn't easy for you."

Don't patronize me, Helen!" Longworthy spat. He was losing his grip on his temper as his frustrations increased. After years of giving orders, he had been forced to take the kind of orders that he wouldn't have believed anyone capable of giving. His guilt at letting his personal convictions cause the capture and torture of his whole family was now compounded by the guilt he felt about the wildly sexual joy he had just experienced with his own daughter. For her to sympathize with him now was another thorn of guilt pricking his hide. He blew up.

"Could it be that you're trying to keep me busy thinking about how I got us all into this, just to knock me off the train of thought you don't want me to follow? You wouldn't want me to wonder, would you, about how accomplished a bed partner you seem to be?"

Helen gasped, shocked at what he was insinuating.

"You're a regular bundle of passion, aren't you? A vixen who loves cock so much she don't care how she has it – even if it's her own flesh, by God!" He was panting as he sputtered the last words.

Helen was sobbing, now She knew again the shame she had felt before as she realized her unnatural passions for her father. But one of the excuses she'd had was that he was a desirable person in so many other ways. She couldn't get excited over just any male. But her father had always been so special. He was so understanding and gentlemanly and solicitous for others. This wasn't like him at all. She felt lost, truly lost for the first time since the whole kidnapping thing had started. She was alone in the midst of her family. The father she'd loved more than anything in the world had turned against her. He hated her.

"*Charles!*" Ruth's voice was like a sharp icicle piercing the thick atmosphere of the cellar. Even in the depth of his angry frustration, Longworthy's ears burned at that address. When she called him Charles, Ruth was not about to agree with anything he said or did. And the coldness of her tone now promised even more than the usual rhubarb.

"If I weren't chained to this darned wall,

I'd come over there and beat you to death with your own pocket watch!" Her tone had not gained any warmth since she first spoke to him.

"This whole family is suffering because they trusted you to do the right thing. I could have raised hell back there at the hotel and insisted you pay the ransom. But I let you make the decisions. And I'm not about to cry on your shoulder now, just because your handling of the affair has landed us here.

"But I'll be damned if I'll have you condemn that girl for having the depth of sexuality she inherited – in part – from you! As did your son! And I admit to at least half of the genes that are responsible for their passionate natures.

"Just what the devil do you think Frank and I were forced to do up there? Play pat-a-cake? We gave in to their threats in pretty much the same way that I imagine you two did. And we did things that mother and son should never in God's world do. And we enjoyed it! Both of us! And we were sorry it happened. And we talked it over like two intelligent, educated, enlightened people should. And we decided not to let it ruin our lives.

"But that could all go by the board. You come along with your self-pity and anger at your own weaknesses and accuse your daughter of habitual promiscuity, and you can ruin all our lives!

"Well, you're not going to do it! I won't let you! This mess is a time for all of us to stick together. And it seems to be a time for revelations, too. Well, let me do a little revealing of my own.

"You seem to be shocked to discover that your daughter is responsive to the stimulation of a healthy male body controlled by a mind that- when it's thinking properly-commands respect and admiration. Would you rather she was a frigid bundle of inhibitions that would go through life looking for a storybook romance that never came?

"And don't tell me that you're unaware of that very normal phenomenon known as a father fixation? Damned few girls don't idolize their fathers, if the men are worth a damn at all. Take a gal like that and force her, naked, into her father's naked arms, and let her feel his naked sex against her very vulnerable body, and what do you have?"

Ruth paused for breath, but not for long. She was fighting for the very foundations of her family, and by its very nature the battle was going against her. It was such an unprecedented situation for any family to find itself in.

"We've been forced to learn a lot about ourselves, and about each other. At least that holds true between Frank and me, and between Helen and you, Charles! And we may not be pleased with what we learn, but we can surely forgive in others the same weaknesses we find in ourselves; and in case there are any doubts, let me hear you right now, Charles Hiram Longworthy, deny before God and your family that you did not find pleasure in the incestuous relationship you were forced into with your own daughter! Go on! Let's hear it for old Charlie!"

Longworthy came apart. He began to heave with great, tearing, gasping sobs as he broke under Ruth's complete spotlighting of his weaknesses. When he could get his breath, he tried to speak.

"God, I'm sorry! Can you forgive me? Any of you?"

"I forgive you Papa," said Helen, and her own tears coursed down her cheeks as deep emotions wrenched at her heart.

"Sure, Pater," said Frank, shakily. "Like Mama says, we all were forced to learn all too much about ourselves. I sure couldn't cast the first stone, the second, or the third."

It was quiet for a minutes then Longworthy dared to ask the question. "Ruth?"

He waited, and as he waited, he thought. Then he knew he hadn't said enough.

"Ruth, I know that I have to ask your forgiveness especially. You gave me the two finest youngsters there are, anywhere, and I've not only let them down, but I've caused them unnecessary misery. And by implying that Helen had gone wrong, and that it angered me, I intimated that it was her mother who was at fault.

"God! I don't know what came over me! Here I am, venting my spleen on the very ones who should be applauded. Most kids would be in shock from having to go through all this, but my whole damn family except me is riding out the storm. I'm not too sure I want to get out of this alive, myself. As long as I can get the rest of you free. I'm not sure I'll be able to live with myself after this."

"Charlie," Ruth's voice came softly to him, and he got up the courage to look over at her for the first time since she'd scalded him with her words. "You've been carrying the load for all of us. Sure, each one of us suffers from all this. But who is it that the other three have been looking to for a way out? Who's been straining his brain to figure out how to protect the people he's always been responsible for? With all you've had on your mind, it took the very worst straw to break the camel's back. I think you've done pretty well. How about it, kids?" In unison, Helen and Frank answered her.

"It'll take more than this to better a Longworthy!" Everyone chuckled at their simultaneous use of the same words. Then, as the laughing died down, Longworthy spoke.

"We'd better make use of whatever time we have left. I think I'm supposed to be dropped off somewhere in Havana in the morning. I'm supposed to get the money, then be brought back here. By the way – the price has doubled. But that's nothing. I hope you all know that it wasn't the money that made me refuse before." They all assured him that they knew that.

"Well," replied Longworthy, "just so you understand that I did what I did because I thought it was the sensible thing to do, based on my own observations of past kidnappings throughout history."

"Papa! Since you know where we are, from my description, you can bring the *policía* back here, can't you?" Helen asked.

"I'm going to have to play it pretty cagey," said Longworthy. "I can't be sure what they might have up their sleeve. I know for one thing, Consuelo has eyes for Frank, and that Fernández has half-promised her she could have him for a playmate once I start for Havana. We've got to think of some way to stop that. Can you imagine that filthy woman getting that close to you?"

"Ugggh!" said Frank, feeling his insides squirm sickeningly. "She made a pitch earlier, when I was washing up in the bathroom – she exposed herself to me. Why would anyone want to be so dirty?"

"We'll probably never know, thank God!" said Ruth. "But we've got to think about how to keep her from contacting any of us. Heaven knows what kind of diseases a Havana whore is liable to carry."

"I'm going to refuse to bring back the money unless she goes along to Havana," said Longworthy. "I'll insist on her accompanying me when they drive me to wherever they're going to let me off. That's the only way I can think of to derail whatever train of thought she has about Frank."

"Where could the big Negro be, I wonder?" mused Frank. "I haven't seen him since be was down here earlier, just before Mama and I were taken upstairs."

"I don't think that Osjami really likes Fernández, although he takes orders from him," said Helen. "Osjami seems to have a conscience, and I think he hates the way Fernández enjoys being sadistic with us."

"Maybe so," replied Longworthy. "But he also could be out somewhere laying some kind of groundwork for tomorrow. After all, they have to plan pretty carefully before they turn me out some place in the city, and they'll probably have me followed while I go to get the money."

"I'm curious about how you're going to

contact them after you get it," Frank said. "They must have something pretty sneaky figured out-after all, you might be suspected of having yourself followed by the *policía* or something."

"I imagine they'll contact me. Probably have me return to the area where they let me off and wait until they're sure I wasn't followed before they reveal themselves."

"However it's done, you can be sure they'll take plenty of precautions to protect themselves," said Ruth. "Be careful every minute, Charlie! Don't take chances!"

"I won't," Longworthy promised. "If I did something stupid, and they decided to kill me, you might all be left here to rot in this godforsaken dungeon. You can bet I'll be plenty careful!"

Chapter 7

As the battered old coach carried him on his blindfolded way to Havana, Charlie was concentrating on the routes and distances. Fernández was driving, and he was seated beside Consuelo inside. He knew that the dim interior of the coach would not permit any perception of his blindfold by those outside the vehicle. Helen had told him about the blinds that could be pulled down to obscure the occupants.

He began orienting himself as soon as the coach started down the lane of the farm, and tried to guess at distances and speeds as they proceeded. By the time he began to catch the sea smells that announced their approach to Havana, he was fairly certain that he knew the entire route he'd travelled.

The old coach came to a halt, and Longworthy's blindfold was removed. He was able to see that they were inside some kind of big stables. The three walls around them were bare. The cobbled floor was covered in hay.

The light which came through the big

door behind them did not penetrate the windows of the coach, but by the smells and sounds Longworthy guessed they were in the waterfront district.

"You will return here in exactly twenty-four hours," ordered Fernández. "And you will wait here until you are contacted. I need not tell you that you will be observed during that time. One of the reasons for the large amount of the ransom we demand is that we have many people in our pay.

"You will go to only those places I tell you. You may go to the bank, of course, where I know you have connections. That is necessary to arrange for the money. And you may stay at your hotel tonight. If you wish to eat at any place other than your hotel, it will have to be *La Bodeguita*. Any other stops will be suspect, and your family will suffer for your attempts to be clever. Understand?"

Longworthy nodded, and then the door opened and Fernández shoved him outside. He just had time to step backward before the coach emerged from the stables with a clatter of hooves and a rattle of wheels into the alley, and sped off into the bright morning sun. He stood there, gathering his thoughts for a few moments. Then he stepped out of the deserted building and looked around. He couldn't recognize the immediate neighbourhood, but the smell and direction of the wind told him which way the harbour lay. From this, he could orient himself, and find his way to the hotel. He decided against taking a cab.

The only plan he had in his mind was still half-formed. And it had a prime requisite: he couldn't be followed! He had to shake off anyone who might be trailing him. They would be prepared to follow him on wheels or horseback, he was sure. The local idea of moneyed Americans almost assuredly would lead them to believe that he'd never walk if he could ride.

So he intended to walk until he had spotted his tracker or trackers or convinced himself that there were none. Then he'd catch a cab and initiate his plan. They might not be prepared for this, and if he could do it innocently enough, they might not suspect anything.

He paced casually down the alley to the street, then turned and headed along the sidewalk, watching from the corners of his eyes and trying not to appear interested in either the people or places around him. Most of the pedestrians at this hour were longshoremen, dock workers, market workers and waggoners. The fishermen had long been gone, out to catch the morning tide and look for the seafood that would feed Havana and other towns on the island tomorrow.

He was specifically trying to detect anyone

who seemed to be on the same route as he, and travelling at the same pace. What was a normal rate of walking speed to an American, he knew, would be inconsistent with the stride of the average Cuban, so it did not take long for him to spot the short, wiry character who appeared to be hurrying on his way to some office.

He'd never seen a Cuban that eager to get to work. Those short legs were really pumping to maintain the pace that the long-legged Longworthy was setting.

He spotted the ideal setup almost a block away. One of the old-fashioned street toilets on the sidewalk was very close to a bunch of dray carts parked at the curb. He assessed the layout as he neared it, and tried to gauge the relative pace at which the pursuer trailed him. He slowed a little as he approached the trucks and the men who moved about them.

Just as he neared the centre of the busy area, he sidestepped into the public toilet. It was accessible from two sides, and he knew that his tail would not dare give away his presence by pulling to a halt and waiting or tracking him inside. He heard the click of the heel plates worn by so many small men as the bloodhound walked on past the iron structure

As expected, he found that the slope of the terrain was such that, if he stayed near the end of the pissoir where he'd entered, the top of his head would not be visible to the pursuer as he got down the street a few paces.

He took advantage of the facilities, and as he mentally counted off the seconds, he urinated into the long trough. When he had counted what he thought was about the right amount of time he backed slowly out of the entrance through which he'd come, keeping the sheet metal bulk of the toilet walls directly centred in line between his own position and the sidewalk beyond.

He reached the mouth of the alley he'd included in his plan, and rejoiced in the accumulation of garbage and crates piled out from the building next to the alley entrance. They electively blocked all view of the distant sidewalk that was not covered by the street toilet farther down.

He dashed up the alley and chuckled to himself. By the time the pursuing Cuban decided that his quarry could not have had such a full bladder as to take all this time, and tracked back to find out what was up, it would be too late. And it had been engineered so that he couldn't be quite sure whether it was intentional. Longworthy may have walked into that block specifically to use the toilet, or may have decided while using the facilities to take a different route.

They couldn't very well get nasty about

this kind of thing.

He hastened through the alley and came out on the next street. As he crossed the street, heading toward a likely place to hail a cab, he slowed to a crawl. Just inside the alley entrance was a strangely familiar spot. His pulse raced, and the hair at the back of his neck bristled as he thought of the possibilities. Then he dashed on into the alley and stopped before the facade. Of the bar that had been there twelve years ago, there was no sign.

But he couldn't resist the feel of the treasure hunt. The memory of that drunken night of sex and celebration came back to him as he entered the dim room that had once been a bright, cheerful bar. There was no sign of Teresa, but a man came down the staircase and asked him in Spanish what he wanted. Behind him followed a full figured woman with merry eyes that were now curious, with a fat brown baby in her arms. There was a flash of guilty recognition in her eyes.

"Ah, Señor. You have come for your package. My god. After all these years. Luckily I still have it."

She disappeared for a few minutes and Charlie was left staring at her husband, who looked away, more resigned than hostile. When Teresa reappeared, she had disposed of her baby and she held a small brown paper parcel that she quickly handed to him.

Charlie could not quite believe his luck and took it, searching for something to give her in return, but she forestalled him by saying, "*De nada. Vaya con Dios, amigo.*"

He started to leave, elated, knowing he'd not been foolish to spend the time on what had seemed such a hopeless long shot. Before he could reach the alley, he heard footsteps approaching. There was no sound of the heel plates, but if that were Longworthy tailing someone, he'd be walking on his toes about now, anyhow. He ducked back into a doorway.

The figure moved into sight and on up the alley. It was a policeman. Longworthy started to move, but caught himself in time. He couldn't take the risk of being spotted talking to the law. He'd have to make contact with them where he couldn't be seen.

He watched as the figure disappeared up the alley, then he unwrapped the pistol and rewrapped it in the handkerchief he carried in his pocket. Then he shoved the pistol into his coat pocket, he returned to the alley and headed in the wake of the now-vanished policeman.

He caught a cab two blocks farther from the spot where he'd intended to hail one. And soon he was at his hotel. The desk clerk looked at him strangely, and then gave him his key.

"There 'as been some concern for you,

Señor Long-worthee," he said. Longworthy wondered why a first class hotel would have desk clerks whose accent was stronger than that of a hoodlum like Fernández. He forced a smile.

"We decided suddenly to take a short trip in the country," he lied, not knowing if if the clerk was on Fernández's payroll. Even if he weren't, Longworthy didn't want anything to occur which might bring the Havana *policía* to the hotel. That would be bad for Ruth and the kids! "They are staying with friends for another day or two. I had to return on business." He smiled again as he headed for the elevator.

The gingerbread grillwork of the iron-caged elevator moved downward past his eyes as the car moved up to his floor. Then he was in his suite, going into every room to make sure that he was alone. Then he took out the revolver to examine it and by briefly spinning the chambers he discovered, to his relief, that it was still loaded.

He went into the bathroom, showered and shaved, performed a few other functions, and then put on some clean clothes. He changed quickly, then went to the telephone room and had the switchboard get the bank for him.

In less than fifteen minutes, he had completed initial arrangements for picking up the funds he requested. He would have to go down to the bank at two o'clock to pick up the money.

Then he flaked out on the bed for a while, resting as he tried to visualize all the possibilities of what might occur in the next twenty-four hours or more. The longer he thought, the shakier he became.

He called room service and ordered up some bourbon whisky and ice. When it came, he poured himself three fingers, and as he sipped at it appreciatively, he thought with guilt of the others, chained in the dank cellar back at the farm.

Chapter 8

It had been so early when Fernández unshackled Longworthy and escorted him up the stairs, that the rest of the family were hardly aware of the procedure until the door at the top of the stairwell closed loudly.

There was a long, uncomfortable silence as each of them felt the finality of the way the morning had begun. All night long, everyone had slept fitfully. The small mattresses that were tossed at their feet at night padded the hardness of the floor, but it could not be said to be plush accommodations for the Longworthys, who were used to luxury.

Now, the three of them were shifting their positions miserably, as they sensed the separateness of their plight and that of the man who had gone to get their ransom. In addition to their apprehension about the outcome of today's events, they were all suffering with the pressure of full bladders.

Just as both Ruth and Helen doubted their ability to hold out a moment longer, Osjami came down and unshackled the two women. He preceded them up the stairs, then herded them to the bathroom, where he stood in the doorway, watching, as they relieved themselves.

Helen had deferred to her mother's seniority, and stood with her legs crossed, waiting to get her turn. After Ruth finished, the younger girl hopped onto the commode, just in time. Osjami laughed, and both of them looked up at him in puzzlement.

He told them, in Spanish, how amusing it was that Americans could not get used to the bidet. There it had stood, all the time, while Helen was bursting, waiting to use the more familiar accommodation her mother had monopolized.

Soon, they were laughing with him, and Helen was reminded again that she felt less than anger towards the big Negro. In fact, she thought that she rather liked him. She recalled with gratitude his attempts to lessen her pain when he'd been ordered to break her hymen.

As long as it had to be a rapist that got my cherry, I'm glad that it was someone with a little feeling for others. Even if that was about the biggest cock any human is likely to have! She gave a shudder as she recalled the way the monstrous tool had probed into her.

Then she saw that Osjami was leading her mother back down the hall, not waiting for Helen to finish. In a few minutes, he came back, just as she was flushing the commode and starting to wash up at the basin. He stood in the doorway as she washed, using a small cake of soap that obviously had been filched from some hotel.

When she had finished, the black man held out a small towel to her. As she dried, she wondered why he had brought it now, after they had been forced to wipe their faces with their hands, then shake off the drops from their hands, each time they had been allowed to wash. Even her mother had just now had to do that.

As she finished, her eyes caught the legend on the towel, and she knew that even that had been stolen. Osjami spoke to her in Spanish.

"I stole it last night. A young lady of refinement, such as yourself, should not be denied so many things she is used to having." He smiled at her, and she realized that-in spite of his hugeness, and the blackness of his skin, he was very handsome by many standards.

"Thank you, *Señor* Osjami. I wish that my mother had been allowed to use it, however." He blinked at her.

"I saved it for you, because I felt that I owed you something I can never repay. Even though I was acting under orders, I did take from you that which you can never replace. I have some guilt because of this."

He had a pained look in his eyes.

"If you did not want to do it, why didn't you refuse?" she asked.

"Manolo – *Señor* Fernández – has knowledge of something I once did. If I do not do as he says, he will see that the *policía* learn of it. And then even if I do not wish to admit it, when I saw the beauty of your perfect body before me, I had a great hunger for you. The two things together: they were too much for me!"

Helen smiled at him sympathetically. And then she thought of something else that perturbed her.

"Where does Consuelo fit into this company? Is she Fernández's mistress?"

Osjami laughed heartily.

"They call her *La Puerca* in San Isidro, where Manolo found her. He would not touch her except with MY *pinga*, as the unfortunate joke tells it. When he is very drunk, and wants to have his cruel amusements, or when he wants it to happen for a special reason, as when he had me show you there in Havana, then he orders me to stick my *pinga* in her. But most of the time, he ignores her, because she disgusts even him. He is not without appreciation for the clean, only without compassion."

Helen thought about this. So, even in

the less than sanitary confines of Havana's backstreets, in the heart of the Havana's section noted for its prostitutes and pimps, Consuelo was named The Filth, or The Dirty Woman. She shuddered as she recalled the sight and odour of what could otherwise be a very pretty and desirable woman.

Then she realized that she was standing here, relaxed, talking as if she were not a prisoner, and that Osjami was eying her with renewed interest. She became a little frightened, as the thought came to her that she was separated from her mother and Frank, and that this big, virile Negro – whatever his kindness and intents – actually had her at his mercy. He had admitted to becoming intoxicated with the sight of her body before. What was to stop him from taking her here and now?

The thoughts rushed through her already confused mind: oh, God! I don't know if I could take another attack by that huge prick! It's so big and beautiful and horrible that it fascinates me, amost hypnotizes me – but it hurt so awfully when he stuffed it into my poor pussy. "If the *Señorita* will confer a kindness upon me, I will try to repay her with every sort of favour that I can." Her eyes widened at his words. What could he have in mind? Oh, mercy! Does he want to impale me with his monstrous manhood, again?

"What do you mean?" she managed to ask.

"I can make no precise promises: the *Señorita* must understand that if Manolo gives me a direct order, I have to obey. But at all other times, I will try to help the *Señorita* and her family, and to do such kindnesses as I can do without Manolo finding out. At the very least, I would rebel the moment he might decide to... to kill you!"

Helen gasped. They had pretty well come to the conclusion that their captors would not want to get involved in murder. But now, Osjami, who surely knew them better than the Longworthys, indicated that there was a possibility of Fernández's wanting them dead! Now she was really frightened. "What do you want me to do?"

"I wish to make love to the *Señorita* gently, to taste the wonders of her body without bringing her pain. And Fernández must not know of it! It must be a secret between us. I believe that he has plans to take you in his own way, and he is very jealous!" Helen thought about this for a moment, and then decided that she had very little to lose, and perhaps much to gain. If she could win the big Negro over to their side – and it seemed possible, since he already had demonstrated his sympathy – they would have that much less to fear in the event anything went wrong. And now that she was taking 'precautions', if the harm hadn't already been done, she stood little risk of anything occurring.

But how could he make love to her without hurting her?

She drew in her breath and smiled bravely at him, knowing that she must make the most of this opportunity.

"I think I would like that, *Señor* Osjami," she half-lied.

He took her hand and led her into the living room, where the sofa-bed was still opened to its most functional position.

"We can hear better from this room when the carriage comes back from Havana," he explained.

Then he helped her undress, and soon she was naked under his hungry gaze. As she watched, he peeled off the simple top clothes he wore, then his underpants.

The magnificent hard flesh of his invader was already firmly saluting her desirability. It poised, cobra like, extended from his dark loins, and pulsing with a life of its own. The uncircumcised foreskin was peeling back without any help as the purplish-red tip swelled within the confinement of its folds. Helen's eyes were wide with awe as it seemed to stare at her balefully.

Weak with a strange mixture of dread and lust, she sank onto the bed, and Osjami's eyes followed the flash of her creamy thighs, and the wink of her pink nether lips as she drew one foot up onto the edge of the bed.

Then he was down on the floor on his knees, and kissing her legs, moving his hungry lips and tongue slowly and wetly up the soft, satin contours of her calves, then her thighs, until his mouth met the first feathery tendrils of her blonde curls. The healthy allure of her youthful, feminine odour drew him to the fleshy lips which lay slightly parted, overhung by a stray wisp or two of the soft, blonde hair.

He placed his lips against one of the fleshy folds, and nibbled at it delicately. As Helen whimpered her surprised excitement, the thickness of the tender fold increased, and the deep pink of her inner flesh, as it became exposed, turned to a dark, purplish red as it filled with the responding flush of her rising passion.

The swelling made the lips part even more obviously, and the slightly lighter hue of the wet flesh beneath them increasingly showed. His lips nibbled up one fleshy fold and down the other, then his tongue snaked out and captured a crystal drop of the lubricant that appeared.

Helen watched in the nearby wall-mirror as Osjami paid homage to her desirability. She thought, suddenly, irrationally, that they made a beautiful tableau together. As his tongue searched out her erect bud, standing in its cozy hiding place at the apex of the fleshy lips, she stifled a hoarse wail of need. He licked at the small hardness until she felt she would go mad.

Then the flow of her juices really began, and he was drinking deeply of her passionate flood, as she whimpered and moaned, then wrapped her legs around his head, hugging to her the source of this maddening excitement.

Then her back arched as she felt the tightening of every nerve and muscle in her body. A shimmering haze filled the air in front of her eyes, and a strange heat flowed through her as a great tremor pulsed from the very centre of her body, reaching every fibre of her being. She relaxed and lay there, gasping for breath.

Osjami gave the delicate blossom a final lick with his long, hot tongue, and then trailed a tingling path up across her belly to the dimple of her navel, where he inserted the exciting probe for a thrilling search of its wrinkled surface.

Quite involuntarily, Helen's hands had been cupping her aching breasts, but now she wanted the feel of his lips on them, the suction of his mouth that might relieve the fullness they felt so painfully.

And now he was there, sucking deeply at each swollen, strawberry nipple, and squeezing the sponges of their erection with lips and tongue.

The hard hugeness of his dark member was thrust against her loins as he leaned over her, and in spite of her passionate involvement, she felt fear that he was going to penetrate her with it.

Then his lips left her breast, and he removed his weight from her. She felt his hands on her buttocks, as he rolled her over onto her belly. And now his hands were under her, dipping at the wet flow that still poured from her openings. He spread the slippery juices up past the bottom of her natal lips, along the crease of her body seam, to the tiny, tight opening of her anus. As his hands spread her creamy buttocks apart, he wet the tight exit with the juices he had robbed from her flowing quim.

Then the head of his monstrous erection was pressing at the rear door of her body! She tried to scream, but her mouth was buried in the bedclothes, and she bit down on the fabric viciously as the unbelievable hugeness of him invaded her rectum!

Oh, God! He's going to penetrate my bottom-hole! It wasn't meant for that! I'm not built to take that giant prick in my... my asshole! Oh-h-h! It hurts something fierce! It was like a white-hot locomotive steaming up the path into her intestines. Her bottom raised up in self defence, trying to ease the tightness of the entrance. But she couldn't get away from the largeness of the invading flesh. It ploughed inexorably into her body, forcing its way through the tender wrinkles of her guts as if nothing could stop it.

Then his hand slipped under her belly and began to massage the wet, pulsating flesh of her firm and swollen cunt lips and the hardness of her erect and burning clitoris.

She felt herself responding to the stimulus, even though the pain of the rectal invasion continued. As his hand moved, slopping the juices around in the heated flesh, she began to move, until all she could feel was a horrendous fullness a swelling, aching, burning fullness that threatened to burst her from within. Then she began to sense the oncome of her orgasm, climbing, working its way through her tortured flesh, until she wanted to scream at the absolute completeness of the sensations that throbbed through her, tearing her asunder with their strength. A hoarse gasp from Osjami told her that he, too, was nearing the point of no return.

She felt the fullness at her blossoming flesh as he thrust two fingers deep into her passage, and then the horribly wonderful swelling of his meaty maleness in her rear as it began to pump his fluids into her belly.

She moaned loudly as the twofold invasion

of her body brought her to the cliff-edge. There was no retreat, and then she fell, gasping, weightless, to the bottomless depths below.

She sensed, vaguely, the withdrawal of his shrinking but still large organ from her bowels. And his fingers retreated from her flowing fountain. Then she lay there, panting, wondering how she had lived through the sheer pain and pleasure of it all.

Osjami's weight was gone for quite a while before she managed to gather enough strength to roll over onto her back. Then she saw that he was not in the room. She wondered if maybe she could make a break through the French doors, out into the garden and across the farmlands to someone who could get help for the them. Then she thought about her father, manoeuvring at whatever plans he might have, in Havana. She might foul it all up if she went off on her own and did anything wild on the spur of the moment.

But she knew that the truth of the matter was that she was too weak, too spent, to attempt anything until she could get back her wind and her strength. The ordeal with Osjami had left her a limp, quivering bundle of sated flesh.

Then he was back in the room, standing over her, looking down on her defenceless body as if he could eat it up in a few bites.

"I apologize to the *Señorita*. I did not intend to enter her from the back, like that. I know it is not easy to accept a man that way for the first time. But I was carried away by my passion when the so delicious juices of the *Señorita* were in my nostrils and on my lips. I hope that I have not given the *Señorita* too much pain."

Helen looked up at him, and noted that his huge, limp organ was dripping water. Obviously, he had retired to the bathroom and washed after the anal engagement. She was still quivering and weak from the terrible onslaught, and he seemed to waver in her gaze as she looked up at him.

She tried to smile, but had no way of knowing whether her facial muscles responded. It was like the time she had been alone at home one weekend, when Papa Longworthy and Mother Ruth were Christmas shopping in New York. She'd been lonely and bored, and had grown bold in her solitude. She'd gotten into the liquor shelves at the back of the bar in the den, and drunk herself into a solitary stupor. She recalled that she had tried to make faces into the bar mirror, and laughed at her inability to command her facial muscles to respond.

Osjami smiled down at her adoringly. Then he sat on the edge of the sofa-bed beside her, and she felt the surprising heat of his flesh as his thigh touched her own. She wondered at the effect this chain of events was having on her mind. She felt absolutely amoral as she lay there, enjoying the play of the mild breeze on her nude body, and the contrasting heat of the black man's flesh against hers.

She rolled over halfway and leaned up on her elbow, then looked at the dark skin of the huge man as he sat there, looking for all the world like an African prince in his nuptial chambers.

He was a clean man, as evidenced by his immediate repair to the bathroom to wash after the episode he'd just completed. And he was a good man, basically, trying to be honest with her, when he really needn't have, because she was absolutely under his power.

She felt a strange tenderness for this big Negro who had just violated the previously inviolable entrances of her body. He had torn her maidenhead several days previously, and now he'd plunged his raping flesh into the tenderness of her anal sphincter. Yet, he had brought her a wild, primeval pleasure in the midst of her otherwise bland existence if one were to discount the sadistic influence of Fernández on the scene.

She leaned over Osjami's lap, inspecting closely the resting length of this flesh that had now battered the tissues of her two most private body openings. It looked so tender and harmless, now, almost as if it were incapable of the ravages it had wrought on her vulnerable body. She leaned over it, looking at the dark skin and the fine lines of the veins that ran through its intriguingly patterned surface. Something came over her that she could not then or later define. It was a compulsion born of her strangely maternal feelings for this big man with the tender heart, and the fantastic pain-pleasure he had given her.

She lowered her head closer and closer to the fascinating display of black and pink flesh. Then her lips touched it, and she felt a deep thrill of combined revulsion and hunger as its softness contacted the sensitive tissue of her lips.

Her hand stole out beneath her poised mouth, and lifted the limpid member. It lay gently, softly, vulnerably on her fingers like a sleeping snake. She brought its intriguingly soft darkness up until it lay helplessly exposed in her palm.

Then she wrapped her lips over it, letting its satin slide through the grip she gently imposed on it. When the tip slipped into her mouth, she tongued it delicately, then made her hand peel back the soft skin from its extremity.

The dark head glided into her mouth, and she made her tongue test every soft, tender spot on its surface. Then she began to suck on it. As she vacuumed its round fullness, it began to swell. In seconds, it had doubled its size, and it was pulsing within her mouth as though it had a life of its own.

Her hand squeezed the base of the stiffening organ, then slid back to cradle the fullness of the wrinkled, hairy scrotum which hung below it. She gently massaged the egg-shaped testicles within, eliciting a series of groans from Osjami.

"*Señorita*! I cannot contain myself! I will spend in your mouth! *Ai! Pinga!*"

He sounded as if he were in pain. She continued to lick at the soft hardness of the glans in her mouth, and then she felt the pressure of his hands on her body, and she was rolled over with him onto the bed. He had spread her thighs in the air, and was licking at the wet heat of her loins with great upward strokes of his broad tongue.

She felt the approach of another strong current sweep through her, and then the fullness in her mouth grew as the pumping, throbbing pulse of his penis filled her mouth and throat. She swallowed the thick sperm-load to keep from choking, and it seemed to fill her forever, then it was over, and she relaxed her lips and jaws as the full tide of her passion carried her over the crest.

When she came to, she kept her eyes closed for a long time. God! she thought.

What have I done? I literally sucked that big cock of his, and he didn't even force me to do it! What's happened to me? As she realized the enormity of her perversion, she started to feel nauseous.

Quickly, she got off the bed and ran out and down the hall into the bathroom. When she had emptied her queasy stomach, she gargled with clear water from the jug, then drank several swallows.

She had half-collapsed onto the bidet, she relaxed a little, and felt the tension decrease as her bladder emptied. Then she summoned up the strength to operate the controls, and flushed herself out with the rushing water.

When she had dried herself, Osjami was standing in the doorway.

"*Señorita* has been more kind to me than I asked. I will do everything to protect her and her family. I shall always remember the joys of today."

He disappeared into the hall, and waited politely until she came out of the room.

When she had been led back downstairs, her mother looked at her strangely, and after the black man had re-shackled her to her chains, Ruth spoke to her.

"What's been going on, dear? He kept you up there a long time after he brought me back."

Helen drew a deep breath, tempted to

tell her mother all, and then thought better of it. She refused to lie, and she couldn't stand the shame of telling what she had done, unforced.

"Osjami and I were talking," she said, revealing the semi-truth. "I think he will try to help us, if he can."

Chapter 9

Charles Hiram Longworthy was sitting at a sidewalk table in front of the approved cafe. *La Bodeguita* was relatively smart. Its facade was a grayish white, with red trim. He noticed that the waiter who brought him his rum and water had dirty nails.

Other than the neglect of his manicure, Pedro – as the waiter had introduced himself – could not be faulted. His courtesy and the speed with which he appeared when required were much better than the American had found in the hotel dining room.

Longworthy listened to the guitarist inside the cafe. He was playing some Spanish love song and singing with that harsh edge to his voice that was so distinctive to the area. The American remembered sitting in sidewalk cafes in 1898 when other tunes were more in vogue. He looked at his pocket watch. Still almost an hour before he was due at the bank.

He'd spent all of this morning in planning and preparing for what was ahead. He unconsciously patted the breast of his jacket, feeling the papers which he'd put in the inside pocket. A rough map of the Cabañas area, pinpointing the farmhouse, a slightly less rough sketch of the floor plan, with suggested approaches for the *policía* when they closed in, and a brief few paragraphs describing the situation there.

He didn't pat his hip pocket where he again carried the Colt. But he could feel its reassuring hardness as he leaned back in the chair. What worried him was the probability that he would be given some kind of search when they picked him up. He argued with himself that he had lost their original bloodhound only for a few minutes. He was sure that they also had the hotel staked out, and that they knew he hadn't had time for any lengthy conversations.

He'd checked the suite, and knew that it had been searched thoroughly during the family's absence, as his small travelling pistol was missing from his luggage. He knew that it hadn't been the *policía*, because the hotel manager would have been bound to inform him. So presumably Fernández and Company wouldn't expect him to be armed. They knew how much cash he had on him – he seldom carried a lot of cash – and the money orders had been in the hotel suite, so they should know he couldn't have purchased a pistol in the short time he'd had after evading their "tail" up to the moment he arrived at the hotel.

Still, they might want to be certain he hadn't acquired a knife or something. Yes, he had to expect that he would be frisked again. He gambled that it would happen after he'd entered the car. He'd try to slip it into the seat while they went over him, then get it back before they arrived at the farmhouse.

He ordered steak and a green salad, and Pedro brought a fine plate of fresh shrimp to start him off. He mentally saluted Fernández's taste in restaurants, as he enjoyed the rest of his meal. He promised to bring the family here after he'd gotten them out of this mess.

He ate slowly, and after he'd paid the cashier, he returned and gave Pedro the most generous tip that he could afford. The man's face creased in gratitude as he thanked Longworthy profusely, begging him to return.

At the bank, *Don* López Famosa took Longworthy through the wooden gate into the plush office area reserved for VIP's. *Don* Lopez was a thin, tall man with graying black hair – a typical 'man of distinction'. He presented the draft for Longworthy to sign, took it to one of the clerks, and returned to sit with his patron until the cash was ready.

Longworthy slipped the papers from his

inside jacket pocket, and handed them to *Don* López.

"Wait until after I leave here, then find some way to get these to the *policía* without being followed. It shows exactly where and how to apprehend the kidnappers who are holding me and my family."

Don López Famosa's eyes narrowed as he accepted the papers, then he put them in the top drawer of his desk.

"I could telephone them and have them send a man over here to get them," he suggested.

"No!" Longworthy insisted. "They may have someone watching the bank who might know the man they send. Better if you phone them and have them pick them up somewhere else after you drop them off in a safe place. We can't take any chances. The leader of this gang is very vindictive, and a sadist. He would enjoy the excuse to torture us more than he has already."

Famosa nodded understandingly.

The clerk arrived with the money, and *Don* López counted it out into the attache case Longworthy had brought with him from the hotel. The moment the case was latched, the American stood up, shook hands with the banker, and thanked him.

"We'll be very grateful for your help in delivering those papers, *Don* López,"

Longworthy said.

"Please call me Juan," said the banker. "I am happy to be of service."

The cab which pulled up as Longworthy came out of the bank could very likely be a plant, he knew. But it didn't matter. All that counted was that he would appear to be following orders. If he conducted himself properly from here on, and came back with the money, they would have little to say about the few minutes during which he'd shaken off his first tracker. After all, he had made it look very innocent and accidental.

When he was again in the hotel, he talked to the desk clerk.

"Do you have a paper cutter in your office that I could use in my room for a while?" he asked. "You mean scissors?" queried the clerk.

"No. A cutter for working with a small stack of paper. Something to cut several thicknesses at once."

"Ah, yes. I believe there is one in the manager's office. I'll send up a boy with it."

"No. I'll take it with me, now. And wrap it before you bring it out of the office. This is a very private matter, and I wouldn't want any of the other members of your staff to know about it."

The clerk looked at him curiously, then disappeared into the manager's office. In a few minutes he came out with a newspaper-wrapped bundle. Longworthy thanked him, then went up to his suite, having first requested that all the newspapers available be sent up to him. Today's and for the previous two days, including the American editions.

The stack which a bellboy brought up later was much larger than Longworthy had expected, and more than he required. He busied himself cutting packs of newsprint into the exact size of the banknotes.

Then he opened the attaché case and laboriously duplicated the packets of money. He placed a genuine banknote on top and bottom of each phoney pack. When he'd completed the project, anyone looking inside the case would believe it to contain exactly what it looked like: a hell of a lot of money.

He took the loose bills which had piled up on the bed, and put them into one of the travel cases which were a part of his wife's luggage, then shoved it under the bed.

He took the remnants and scraps of newspaper into the bathroom and tore the larger pieces until they could be flushed down the big drain. After he'd erased all the evidence of his trickery, he rewrapped the paper cutters went back down to the desk, and returned it to the clerk, who carried it back into the office.

Longworthy then went to the lobby and

pretended to browse the magazines for a while, after which he went back up to his room.

He was thinking about the timing of the events to come, as he undressed and got into bed. If he could get to sleep this early, he'd be up very early, refreshed, and able to think fast when the time came. What bothered him was whether the *policía* would do as he asked, and wait until he'd been taken back to the farmhouse before closing in. He wanted to be there with the family, in case of anything unforeseen.

He dreaded the first moments following his return. If Fernández looked at the money packets closely, there would be trouble. But he hoped that he could convince the Cuban that he wasn't trying to be cheap and greedy. He just wanted the payoff to be on his own terms.

If Fernández would let the others go back to the hotel suite, then phone him, Longworthy would remain at the farmhouse under captivity as hostage, and when he was convinced that Ruth and the kids were safe and could not be recaptured, then he would tell Fernández where to get the money. He planned to wait until Ruth sent word from the hotel suite, make sure from her that they were safe, then have her get the money from the suitcase under the bed, and have a bellhop or other messenger deliver it to wherever Fernández wanted it.

He tossed for quite a while, and was just getting drowsy enough to sleep when a bellhop delivered a note to his door. It was a scrawled message from Fernández.

"The schedule has changed. Bring the money down and get into the cab which is waiting for you in front of your hotel. You have five minutes. Hurry. Fernández"

Longworthy started to worry. Things were bad, this way. The *policía* would not come to the rescue until late in the morning! He'd better be able to convince Fernández about the phony money!

When he came out of the hotel, a cab pulled up from the rank and opened its door. He got in; the driver set off into the traffic without asking the destination, so Longworthy sat there quietly, expecting to be driven to the stables where he'd been dropped.

But within ten or twelve blocks, the cab stopped at the curb. The battered old black coach pulled up beside it, and Fernández got out and paid the cabbie. Longworthy was hustled into the coach, and they drove off. Someone he didn't recognise was driving, and the sadist was seated beside the American, who wondered why he wasn't being blindfolded.

When they were well on the road to Cabañas, he turned and looked at Fernández, noting the tight corners of the Cuban's mouth, and the way his eyes were narrowly slitted, even though only a little light entered the covered windows. "No blindfold?" Longworthy finally asked.

"Of what use would it be to a man who can map the route we take and diagram the house to which we go?" The Cuban's voice was hard and sharp, and it made a warning bell ring in Longworthy's mind. "I beg your pardon?" he asked.

"You heard me quite well, *Señor* Longworthy. Let us not play any more games with each other. You have tried to enlist the aid of the *policía*, and you have failed. You have attempted to double cross me and you have failed. Let us see if you have the money." He pulled the attaché case onto his lap and opened it, then stared down at the packets for a moment before he closed the case.

"At least in this you have not failed. It is the only thing which has saved you and your family from a number of unpleasant experiences. Now, move forward in your seat, while I see if you have brought with you anything we would not want you to have in your possession."

Longworthy put his hands behind him as if to push himself forward. He pulled the Colt from his pocket, and almost decided to use it there and then. But Fernández's own gun was aimed at him. He tucked the Colt behind the seat cushion and scooted forward. The Cuban used his free hand to feel and pat around for a few moments, then he leaned back and kept the gun aimed at Longworthy.

"Pull out your pockets, one by one, while I see what you have." Longworthy obeyed, and when he had exhibited the contents of every one of his pockets, including the lining itself, the Cuban lowered the pistol slightly. "*Bien.* Now sit back in your seat and relax."

They drove on, and Longworthy studied the countryside, remembering the times he had driven through it in during the war. He wished that his reflexes were as fast now as they had been in those days. And that he had been sharp enough to guess that Fernández might have recruited someone at the bank, for it had to be that which had tipped him off. Whoever it was undoubtedly had followed *Don* López Famosa and grabbed the papers before the *policía* picked them up. It was a hell of a note!

His only hope now was that *Don* López might have studied them before he dropped them off. And that the *policía*, having missed the pickup, would check back with the banker and get enough information to find the place.

When they pulled up in front of the farmhouse, Fernández forced him out of the coach before he could manage to get the Colt back into his pocket. He barely had time to shove it down far enough behind the cushion to hide it from the Cuban, who stayed inside until Longworthy was clear of the vehicle.

The hidden gun had been his last hope to turn the tables by himself. If the *policía* didn't come through, the Longworthys could be tortured to death!

Damn! Damn! Why the hell did I fool with that phoney money? I only wanted to get Frank and the girls out of there before the shooting started between Fernández and the *policía*. Now, it looks like I've killed us all!

All the way down to the cellar, Longworthy was sweating cold drops that beaded on his brow and upper lip. It would be only a matter of time before the newsprint 'banknotes' would be discovered.

When the family was again alone in their dungeon, he confessed to the faulty planning and warned them of what might happen. He couldn't let them have any false hopes, and he was so disgusted with himself for having come a cropper, that he wanted them to hate him for it as he was hating himself. "Exactly where is the gun, Pater?" asked Frank.

"What difference?" Longworthy countered. "We can't reach it from here!"

"Mother gave me a hairpin they missed when they frisked us. I've been practicing, and I can open every one of my cuffs excepting the one on my right wrist. I lock them all up again, each time, just so I won't get caught at it before I'm completely loose."

"I'll be damned!" said Longworthy. "Listen. Keep working on that stubborn one until you get it. If one of us can get loose and get out of here, we'll have it made."

"I know! I know! It's just that I can't seem to do as well when I'm working with my left hand. But I'll keep after it, all right!"

"Fine then. Well, you all should know, anyway. Just in case. The gun is exactly like the old Colt Peacemaker I have at home. You've all had training in how to use it. It's tucked between the seat and seat-back of the carriage. The safety's on. If any one of us manages to get to it, remember this: besides the round in the chamber, there are only five others. So make your shots count if you have to use it on these bastards."

"I'd hate to think of Osjami getting hurt or killed, Papa," Helen interjected.

"What are you talking about?" said Longworthy. He was shocked to hear her defend the black man. "Isn't he the sonovabitch that raped you first?"

"Yes, Papa, but he was acting under orders. Fernández has something on him, and if he doesn't cooperate, Fernández will turn him in. He's really the only one of the bunch who has any compassion at all. And he's really a lot more intelligent and humane than you might guess from the way he acts."

"Helen, honey, you're inclined to romanticize a little too easily, you know. But even if you're one hundred percent correct in your opinion of the Negro, we can't take chances. All of our lives depend on getting the upper hand with these people."

"Yes, Papa, but he's promised to help us all he can. He doesn't dare do anything that Fernández might discover and use as an excuse to turn him over to the *policía*. But in any other way, I really believe that he'll help us. He just can't refuse a direct order from Fernández if he's likely to be found out."

"What if Fernández orders him to kill us?"

"Oh, Papa! You don't think they'll go that far, do you?"

"Honey, we are very likely to be skating right now on thinner ice than ever before in our lives – and I hope we can get lucky enough to get out of it somehow!"

"Well, the worst thing that Fernández can be holding over his head is murder - right? He wouldn't commit one murder just to keep from being turned in for another, would he?"

"Of course, he would! He'd have to! Whatever Fernández has on him – even murder – is unknown to the authorities at present. If he had to kill us on Fernández's orders, that could be presumed to be without the knowledge of the authorities, too. What he really has to fear is Fernández's telling on him. And that will happen, supposedly, the moment he refuses to do anything Fernández orders including our mass murders!"

"I think he'd kill Fernández, first!" said Helen. "I really do!"

"Well, sweetheart, we can't take chances. The only thing we can do is plan to overcome them, no matter how we do it. If Osjami goes along with our takeover – if we are lucky enough to make it – then he'll be spared. But if he resists us, we'll have to fight him in any way we can. It's called survival, my dear. Surely you can see that."

"I guess so," said Helen, feeling strangely sad about this discussion that might lead to the kindly black man's death.

They ceased any further discussion as the stairway door opened. Fernández descended slowly, and as he entered the circle of light provided by the oil lamp in the centre of the arena, they saw the black look he wore on his face. "It seems that we have need of the services of Madame Longworthy," he announced. He moved to where Ruth was chained, and unlocked her shackles. He led her up the stairs as the others looked at each other and then followed the departing pair with anxious eyes.

Ruth was taken to the living room, where the sofa bed was opened and ready for occupants. She looked at it, then studied the dark face of Fernández.

"Your husband has seen fit to play a dangerous game," he said. "I have examined the ransom he brought from Havana, and it seems to be somewhat less than the agreed amount." He was looking at her with mocking eyes, and the arch of his brows made her think of the prototype of all the Mephistopheles characters she had seen or imagined in the role.

"We shall now begin a very interesting series of adventures. You are honoured to be the first member of your family to inaugurate this series. Take off your clothes and get on the bed!"

The elegant millionaire's wife slowly removed her clothes, wondering what was going to happen to her, now. When she had removed all but undergarments, she hesitated, wondering again what she was in for. Fernández stepped toward her, and tore the scant coverings from her, making the straps cut her shoulders and arms, cruelly.

Then his hands were under the band of her bloomers, and he gave the material a mighty jerk downward, ripping them from the area of her blonde-feathered genitals, and off her thighs. Another jerk, and he had them down past her calves, at her ankles. She stepped out of them, and her eyes were wide as he manhandled her rudely back onto the bed. Then he was spreading her legs, and his mouth found her opening blossom of flesh, as it split asunder.

He's eating me. I hope it ends these! What can he have planned? Oh! he certainly knows how to get at the heart of a cunt! He's licking and slurping at my little erection as though he's going to devour it! Oh-h-h! That tongue! It's pushing right into my hot pussy! What's he doing, now? Oh-h-h-h! He's biting at my cunt lips with his teeth! Oh-h-h! It hurts so *good!* This is torture, all right, but I think I can stand it, of I can just hold on!

Then she felt the lips and tongue depart, and her hungry flesh lay there, exposed and throbbing with her need. Suddenly she felt the entrance of a hard intruder, as Fernández's rigid member penetrated her passage.

He's fucking me, now. I can stand that. I have taken 'precautions' this morning, and I can take whatever he dishes out. In fact, I think it feels good!

Then the man's cock was pounding at her, and she felt the slap of his hairy bag on her buttocks and anus as he plunged repeatedly into her depths. She began to groan as the frictional contact of his loins rubbed her sexual extremities in the most thrilling way.

Then he was moving faster, and she felt his mouth on her breast. He sucked and nibbled at the delicate bud, which hardened under his teasing mouth. She felt herself about to spend, and the thrilling plunge into oblivion was an ecstatic pleasure, until he started to bite her. As she felt the shuddering tremors start to spread from the centre of her being, his teeth clamped down on her tender nipple, and she felt pain such as she'd never known before.

Then he was grabbing her buttocks with his pinching hands, clawing his nails into her soft flesh until she wanted to die from the agony. Her scream started deep in her throat, and rolled out loudly onto the afternoon air.

He reached up with one hand and grabbed her by the throat, cutting off her sounds at the source. But the teeth didn't let up. They bit deeply into the sensitive flesh of the spongy nipple, and the shock travelled through her like an electric current.

Fernández was speeding up his movements still more, and she felt the beginnings of his pulsing end.

He's spending in me, and I hurt so much that I can't spend with him! God! He's a heartless beast! I'm hanging high and dry, and I'm about to lose out while he fills my helpless cunt with his hot spunk. He's a bastard – worse than I imagined! And I thought Cubans were great lovers. Oh-h-h! Fuck me some more, and stop that biting!

But she was out of luck. Fernández was only out to relieve his animal lusts, and to make her miserable. She was furnishing the first payment on what he felt Longworthy owed him for the double-cross!

He was grabbing her buttocks tightly, pulling her to him, as he pumped his heated fluid into her in spasms. The flow was still filling her, and she realized it, but she was dying for a release of her own. He rolled off her, and she felt the wet trail his member left across her thighs.

She looked up as his weight was lifted from her, and he got to his feet, and disappeared from her sight. She could see in the wall-mirror the results of his attack. Her left breast was streaked with blood, and the nipple was still bleeding slightly. The streak of white, stringy semen that trailed across her thigh from the pinkly wet slit of her opening was also visible.

She reached down and wiped it off, then smeared it onto the bed-linen in a far corner remote from her head. As she looked up to see what was going on, the gigantic figure of Osjami filled her field of vision.

He was stripped for action, and the hugeness of his member was all she could see. It was stretched to full length and seemed to be throbbing and pulsing as it stood there, extended from the blackness of his loins. Its own darkness seemed to threaten her, and yet she felt no real fear. It seemed large, but her hungry passage was unfulfilled, and anything that would fill her needs would gratify her, now.

Heavy, large hands grasped her buttocks, and she was rolled over onto her belly. The same large hands pulled at her soft skin, around the stomach area, and her behind rose in the air, until she felt the firm cheeks spread by searching fingers.

She turned her head, and looked into the wall-mirror. She could see the giant black man poised over her, and his hands separating her buttocks. Then one of his hands disappeared under her, and she felt the fingers probing at her flowing crotch.

He's dipping his hand into my cunt, but only for the juice, she thought. What's he doing? Then she felt the wetness on the tight circle of her virgin anus. My God! Even Charlie hasn't fucked me there! My ass is too tight! That horrendous cock of his will split me in half!

Then she felt the head of his weapon press at the tight ring of her anus. Its heat and hardness seemed to tolerate no resistance. She felt her tissues burn, parting as the stiff invader pressed ever harder at the tender ring of flesh. A monstrously swelling sensation began to spread through her as his bulk slowly forced its way past the tight, puckered exit he was using as an entrance.

The aching pain of it was unbelievable. The force of the huge intrusion violated her with steady, brutal pressure. She was being spread open where she had never before been touched.

"Stop! Please stop! I can't stretch there like this! Fuck me right! You're killing me! Oh-h-h!" She was gasping with the agony of her fullness. Then she started to pass out. As her muscles automatically relaxed, the pain lessened, and she started to come to before completely losing consciousness. This made her tighten up her muscles, again, and the pain increased.

Oh! I've got to relax. It helps to relax, but I can't! Oh, God! There's no use begging. They're going to hurt us as much as they can. *Ooh-h-h!* Now he's fingering me. Yes, that helps. The way he's digging around in my sloppy pussy, helps take my mind off the pain. Oh! Not enough, though. God! That hurts! He's pumping at me, now. It burns so! His finger's in my cunt so deep, too. Oh! It's like being fucked by two cocks at once! If he wasn't so big it might feel good. Oh, if he only weren't so god awful *big!* Osjami was thrusting at her hard, and she could feel the wet slap of his giant ball-sack against her parted cheeks as he banged against her. It felt as if he must have torn up everything inside her. Then his arm, which was around her lower belly, shifted as he changed the position of his hand. In addition to the long finger which was sunk deep into her passage, another finger or thumb now was splashing in the soup of her flowing flesh to massage her throbbing bud. It felt so good that she started to move her hips. She was on her knees, and as she reacted to his stimulating fingers, the movement also gave added impetus to his unorthodox penetration.

Suddenly his size within her seemed to increase. It swelled and pulsed deep in her bowels.

He's spending in my ass. That hot cream is flooding my guts. It's like being fucked by a stud horse and... the most satisfying bowel-relief ever... both at once! *Oh-h-h!* Now I'm spending, too!

Then a red, shimmering curtain closed her off from the outside world as the big, black organ pumped its load into her body. Her flesh seemed to separate from her mind, melting into blobs of wet, hot, red meat that gleamed fluorescently in the blackness of space.

In a series of colourful explosions, she lost consciousness.

Chapter 10

The return to the dungeon was different this time. Fernández had thrust her clothes at her-minus the torn bra and panties-and told her to dress. There was no time to clean up. He let her stop just long enough to urinate on the commode, then pulled her off and forced her down the hall to the stairs.

She could walk only with difficulty, and going down the steps was a painful ordeal. When she had been shackled in place, the Cuban unlocked Frank and shoved him toward the stairs. As the boy began the upward climb, Fernández leered at Longworthy over his shoulder, and spoke as he followed Frank on the stairs.

"Madame has been well-fucked for you, *Señor*, at front and back doors. Later we will bring her up and give her something to eat. A lot of meat and a little gravy!" He laughed maniacally as he disappeared through the stairwell, and the door closed in the middle of his mad gurgles.

"God! Ruth, I'm so sorry for you. I'm such a dumb sonovabitch for getting us into this mess! If I could just get my hands on that sadistic bastard for ten seconds!"

"Don't, Charlie! It won't help to berate yourself. And don't feel so bad about me. After all, I'll soon heal up. We have to keep our minds occupied with planning and scheming. We don't have time for recriminations and worrying about individual problems. There's only the one problem-getting loose, somehow!"

"I know. You're right, Ruth. If only Frank can get that last lock picked, we'll stand a chance."

"Mother," Helen said, "it might help to know that you'll stop hurting sooner than you expect to."

"Helen! Do you mean that you were ... that they ..."

"Yes. Osjami got me from the back, too. It hurt like anything, but it's not so bad now. Although it burns for a while, every time I ... I mean ... I think I'm going to eat awfully light for a few days, to ease any additional problems."

"You poor kid!" Longworthy groaned. "These maniacs all ought to be killed. They're a menace to the whole damned world!"

"I wonder how poor Frank's making out?," Ruth said.

* * *

Frank wasn't making out as well as he might.

He was flat on his back on the sofa-bed, and Consuelo's mouth was working on him. She'd started on his belly, worked her way juicily down to his thighs, then back up to his slowly responding genitals.

She's a filthy animal, but she sure knows how to stir a guy! That tongue of hers must be twice as long as normal, and it manoeuvres about like an anteater's! He felt it swirl around the end of his organ and then seesaw across the tip like a fleshy file. Damn! That tickled and almost hurt at the same time.

Then she had the greater part of him in her mouth, and began to strip it in long strokes, sucking deeply each time she neared the tip. Oh, God! That crazy college pal and his story about the milking machine! It couldn't have been any worse than this! Nothing could be worse. I can't stand it!

But there was worse to come: Consuelo pulled her dirty skirt up around her middle and swung her unbathed body onto the bed until her legs straddled Frank's chest. She hadn't let go the captive flesh with her mouth for a second! Then she backed herself into position and shoved her hairy bush into Frank's face. The smell was overpowering!

Was it only two days ago that he had found himself surprised by his enjoyment of the faintly pissy, musk like scent he'd discovered between his mother's legs? Somehow, he reasoned, that had seemed a healthy male reaction.

But nobody could be attracted by this! The red wetness suspended over his face was dripping with the girl's excitement, and the drops struck him on the nose and mouth. Then she lowered it on target! The wet heat of her flesh smothered him. He rolled his face away and spat at the wall.

Then his right hand was grabbed, and Fernández's glowing small cigar tip was pressed against his wrist! He yowled loudly before he could close his mouth. He hated showing his pain.

"You will cooperate with Consuelo, or you will be a mass of blisters when we take you back downstairs!" the Cuban promised.

Frank wondered which he could stand the longest-the burning or the sickening flesh in his mouth. He tried to think clearly through the smarting pain on his wrist. He had to stay in condition so he'd be able to help with an escape. He'd have to force himself to do whatever they ordered-for now. But if he got half a chance, he'd make them pay for it!

The slimy flesh pressed again to his mouth, and he nibbled at it halfheartedly. She rotated her hips, making the wet meat move on his mouth. When the surprisingly

large, hard bud of her passion had rubbed up against his lips, she held it there and wiggled to massage it against him.

"Lick it Frank-ee! Suck it for me!" the said, removing her own mouth from him just long enough to get out the words. The initial shock of her odour and wetness at his face had softened his manhood, but now she was awakening it again. As it stiffened in her mouth, he tongued her and sucked at the stiff flesh between his lips.

She was humming as he treated her, and the vibration of the sound drove him wild as her lips encircled him. The rhythm of her oral movements became faster, and he tingled all over as she seemed to pull at his nerve centres.

He could tell that she was getting more excited, too. The juices flowed liberally from her large, open gap, and she was wiggling in the same fast tempo as she was using at the other end. Then she lifted her head to yell at him

"Stick it in me! Put your tongue in me, deep! Quick!"

He reluctantly thrust his tongue into her sloppy passage, and it seemed to suck and swallow at him. Then he felt it go into her until his teeth were pressed roughly against the fleshy outer lips of her canyon, and she wriggled excitedly, frictioning snugly on his lower lip and chin.

Then he was spurting his soul out through his loins, and Consuelo was pumping at him hungrily, sucking at his tip with each stroke, until he felt completely drained. But still she wouldn't stop. She pulled and sucked at him until he thought he'd go mad. When he could take it no longer, he risked another cigar burn. He bit her as hard as he could on a fleshy, swollen lip of her womanhood.

She let go of him and rolled off, laughing with glee.

"I take more than you have to give, no? Even a healthy young man like you will have to have a rest before you can make enough to feed me again! But I am better than you. Even now I am ready for you to suck me so nice some more. Can he, Manolo?" She turned to look at Fernández pleadingly.

"Later. Osjami, take him down and bring up Papa."

"Just one minute, Manolo. Please?" Before Frank could get up, she rolled him over on his belly and parted his buttocks with her fingers. Then her tongue dug into his anus and wiggled hotly. It was a wild sensation! But the thought of what she was doing made him nauseous.

She probed and licked at him, washing the ring of his exit until he groaned with the unexpected ecstasy of it. Then she let him go, again laughing happily.

The Negro motioned at him, and he went back to the cellar, after slipping into his clothes.

"The blister on my wrist ... do you have to use the cuff? I can't go anywhere with the other three locked." Frank's pulse beat swiftly as he awaited the black man's reaction.

Then Osjami nodded, slowly, as he locked only the three shackles. When Longworthy was released, he winked surreptitiously at Frank as he turned to precede Osjami up the stairs.

As he was shoved into the living room, Longworthy saw the gleaming eyes of Consuelo boring into him.

He started to strip on Fernández's command, and the girl peeled off her dirty skirt and blouse. For the first time, he saw that she was really a pretty girl with a superb figure.

But when she threw her naked body on him, the brief admiration was dissolved by the scent of her unwashed skin. She forced a hard breast against his mouth, cupping the globe with one hand as she tried to manoeuvre the nipple tip between his lips.

"Frank-ee, he suck me good! You have more experience, no?"

The revulsion rose up in his throat, and he swallowed, hard. But his lips did not open.

Fernández's small cigar tip against his left buttock made them open as he gasped, but his teeth were clamped together in agony. Nevertheless, Consuelo had wiggled the rising tip of her nipple between his lips, and was cooing in his ear.

"Chew eet for me, gently. Make eet hurt a leetle for me, no?"

Having earned his battle scar, Longworthy slowly obeyed. He wanted to make this last as long as he could stand it, to give Frank as much time as possible to get free. But if he got too many of those burns especially if any of them were in the wrong places and serious enough, it might hamper him in aiding the boy when the time came.

He nibbled with his teeth at the dark, spongy flesh, and Consuelo moaned as he chewed. Then she made him switch to the other breast, and he gnawed at its springy peak until she was gasping. Her body slithered over him, and she grasped his cock and began to stroke it.

When it filled her hand stiffly, she arched her back and scooped her hips downward. Her hot, dripping maw gulped at him and began to engulf him. Her passage was like a throat, and he could feel it swallowing him. Her cunt felt like grasping hands, pulling at him, drawing him in.

Good Lord! What a machine! Millions

must have fucked her for her to get that kind of muscle tone! She sure has an educated pussy! It's milking me like I was a cow's teat!

As she moved her hips above him, squeezing his rigidity with her practiced muscles, she covered his mouth with hers. He got a quick blast of her garlicky, but otherwise sweet, breath and then her hot tongue was plunging into his mouth. She sucked at his lips and probed with her tongue until the expertness of her treatment broke him down despite his distaste.

She vacuumed his tongue up into her mouth and sucked at it as her hips rotated and her buttocks rose and fell above him, pulling and swallowing at his manhood.

Raped, by damn! I'm actually being raped. After all the times I've joked about it, I'm being fucked against my will! Fucked? Hell, I've been fucked by what I thought was the greatest. I'm being milked and that's all you can call it. Her cunt must be a living lake. The juice is all over me!

She worked at him faster as her own excitement built. Then she turned into a fiery tornado. His stretching flesh was caught in the vortex of the sexual cyclone, and it felt as if it were being pulled out by the roots! She was sucking his tongue deep into her mouth as she pressed tightly against him and shuddered. Her whole body shook with her tremors, and it was as if something deep in her cuntal passage wrapped an iron hand around the tip of his wand and squeezed at it.

He spurted copiously into her in violent spasms; they shuddered together for several long seconds.

Consuelo's weight lifted from him, and he rolled to the edge of the bed to get up.

"Wait! We are not through," Fernández said. "Consuelo, lie down on the bed. We are going to have a special soixante-neuf party." The girl stretched out, this time with her feet at Longworthy's head.

"Perfect, *Señor*. Now you get the pleasure of eating Consuelo's very hot pussy. Climb over her and get started!"

"Hell, make her take a douche, first, at least!" demanded Longworthy.

"You are in no position to dictate terms," replied Fernández. His tone was deadly, and so was the look in his eyes. He was moving toward Longworthy, and blowing on his small cigar as he approached.

"You're all crazy! Filthy, crazy-mad animals!" Longworthy muttered. But he climbed aboard just in time to avoid the little cigar's kiss of fire. So he thought. But as he positioned himself over the dirty brunette, he felt its fire boring into his thigh in back.

"There will be no more angry words from you, *Señor*. Or you will go back to the cellar looking as if you had the plague. Do you have any idea how many places I can burn you with one cigar?"

Longworthy was boiling, and the blister rising on his thigh was agony. He steeled himself to what was coming, then tried to hold his breath as he dove into her wet, hairy canyon with his lips. Her head was hanging over the edge of the bed, so he had to stand his toes on the floor and lean his thighs against the edge to poise over her in the proper place. She spread herself wide for him, and the first breath he had to take was pungent. But he had to admit that a large portion of the odour comprised the smell of his own semen, which had flowed heavily into her, and was dripping at her fleshy opening in whitish strings.

It's not bad enough to have to suck on this whore's cunt! I have to eat my own spend. Makes me a second-hand cocksucker. Wait until I get my hands on these swine, I'll make them sorry they were even born!

Suddenly he was shocked at the slimy, wet feel of something in the crack between his buttocks. A hand had slipped into the crease and deposited something greasy there. Now what? Did this dirty whore park her chewing gum in my asshole?

But he found out all too soon that Consuelo was blameless. Hands separated his firm, muscular cheeks, and something hard pressed at his anus.

"Give it to him, Osjami!" Fernández shouted, and Longworthy felt the muscle tissue around his tightened ring stretch as the hardness pressed at the greased, puckered flesh. Then he swelled inside as the fullness entered him.

Bastards! Dirty, filthy animals! They haven't done enough to me already-now I get fucked in the ass to boot! He was so mad that he bit Consuelo's swollen entrance, and she wailed her surprise. Longworthy expected another blister, and tensed him self for it. But he got his punishment in another way. Consuelo wrapped her arms around his waist and took the head of his penis in her mouth.

She bit on it, and he gasped in pain. Then she started to lick it, and in seconds he had another stiff problem. The pain of the bite increased when he swelled up, and it throbbed like a toothache. She worried it with her tongue and lips as he started to carry out his orders again.

He lapped his tongue in the flowing fountain of her red flesh, and she thrust up her hips to meet him, smearing her juices and the leftover semen on his lips, chin and face. He abandoned all restraint and determined to get it over with. He licked at her outsized stiff clitoris until she writhed under him with ecstasy, sucking hard on him as she moaned around the mouthful of his flesh.

The black man was plunging into his bowels up to the hilt, and each stroke ended with a smack as the huge balls slapped against Longworthy's own. Each thrust forced his own organ hard against Consuelo's mouth and throat, but she seemed to take it without too much discomfort. At least, her attentions to him did not slow down.

Then Osjami let loose his loins, and the warmth being discharged in Longworthy's bowels triggered his own lust. He sucked and lapped at the meat below him, then sunk his tongue deep into her passage.

Consuelo moaned heavily around her mouthful of flesh as she began to shudder out her climax. Longworthy's flow pumped into her mouth and throat. He could feel her swallowing, as the head of his tool touched the back of her throat. It coaxed an additional flow from him, and he felt utterly drained.

And still she sucked at him, still more, seeming to draw his guts right out through the tip. It felt like he was dying. As she sucked a last, long string out of him, the black man pulled his limp member from Longworthy's battered anal ring.

The combined feeling was like genuine death from fatigue. Longworthy fell over on the bed and lay there. He couldn't move a muscle. If his life depended on it, he couldn't have gotten up by himself.

Fernández's laughter was filling the room, as he revelled in the ultimate humiliation of this American millionaire who had refused to meet ransom demands.

"Wait!" he yelled at Osjami, who was leaving the room. "Don't go yet. We are going to get the camera for the next step. I am going to have a picture of this rich *Yanqui maricón* sucking your big dirty *pinga*!"

"Manolo!" Even Osjami was shocked now. "Let me wash it off."

"No! To use his own native phrase, I have taken enough shit off this man. Now I will see him take a little of his own shit off you. And get my prize picture at the same time. Consuelo, get the camera and tripod."

"Consuelo is not going to move," said Frank from the doorway, as he calmly took aim and shot Fernández in the kneecap.

Chapter 11

The Cuban's screams filled the room. They sounded loud enough to be heard in the dungeon. Longworthy thought of this, and imagined what the girls might be going through, not knowing who had been shot.

He moved carefully away from the bed, staying out of Osjami's reach, until he got to the lamp table where Fernández had placed his pistol; he checked it to see if it was loaded, then kicked off the safety.

"Very good, Frank. You can get the girls loose, now. Fernández, toss him the keys!" The Cuban was moaning between clenched teeth, as he held the shattered knee in both hands. The artery had not been hit, for the blood was only seeping slowly between the white-knuckled fingers.

"They're already loose. I picked their locks before I went out for the gun. I figured that they could wait at the top of the stairs and trip anyone who showed up before I got back with this."

"That was taking a risk, son. But good work, anyhow. But we still want those keys."

Silently, Osjami moved a hand up to his shirt pocket, and pulled out a ring with one small key on it. He held it out to Frank.

"Use mine," he said. Longworthy and Frank both had covered him with their guns as he reached for his shirt pocket. Now they relaxed.

"How about your key, Consuelo?" Frank asked. She shrugged her shoulders and nodded toward the back of the house.

"In my purse on the table back there." Her eyes were tired, but they showed no fear.

"Good, Consuelo. Now get down there on the floor and get Fernández's key from him." She looked at Frank, and then grinned.

"There are only the two keys." Her accent was less pronounced, now, as she spoke slowly, without excitement.

Frank looked at his father, who nodded at him, then at Consuelo.

"Let's go, Consuelo. The Colt motioned her up onto her feet, and she preceded Frank down the hall. Longworthy heard two short raps, then three more harder raps on the cellar door. He grinned to himself as he thought of Frank planning the signals with Ruth and Helen.

The women came down the hall, but Longworthy motioned them back.

"Stay out of here. Keep to the back of the

house, until these bastards are under chains."
The girls disappeared back down the hall and
he heard them using the bathroom.

When Frank returned, he looked to his
father, then at Osjami, then at the moaning
Fernández.

"We'll do it the easy way," Longworthy
said. You go down first and wait for us. Stay
clear of the bottom of the stairs, in case
Osjami drops his burden. Alright, pick him
up and take him down there!" The revolver
centred on the black man's belly.

He stepped over to Fernández and amid
much groaning and protesting, picked up
the smaller man and started down the hall.
Longworthy followed at a discreet distance,
all the way to the cellar.

Osjami put his load down by the wall
where Frank stood, pointing with the Colt.
Osjami saved them trouble. He walked over
to another set of shackles, then fastened them
around his own ankles and wrists. There was
only resignation on his face.

Frank checked the locks on the black man,
then he and his father got the cuffs locked on
Fernández.

"I have to have a doctor!" the Cuban
protested. I could bleed to death! You could
not have that on your conscience!"

"Oh couldn't I?" asked Longworthy. He
regarded the deflated sadist with disgust.

"You're not bleeding that much. If you're smart, and hold that leg still, you'll be alive when we get you a doctor. If you move it, a piece of that bone or cartilage might just puncture an artery."

"You did not have to shoot me! I wasn't even holding my gun."

"Be thankful you weren't. Frank's a crack pistol shot. He knew that if he'd just threatened you with it, you might have gone for a gun, and he'd have had to shoot to kill. You see, we aren't taking any chances on the safety of our family with a madman like you. Now, shut up and consider yourself lucky."

Frank had gone upstairs, and now he returned with Ruth and Helen in tow. The girls had cleaned up quite a bit, but they still showed signs of fatigue and the ordeal they'd been through.

"I guess we'll have to go into Cabañas and contact the *policía* there, Pater," said Frank.

"I'll tell you what. You keep your eye on things here, and I'll go get the law, and bring some clean clothes for everyone. I know the girls won't want to go back to town looking like they do now." The wry smiles and nods told him he'd been right. "Don't forget the doctor!" groaned Fernández.

"I'd like to," Longworthy told him, then he kissed Ruth, patted Helen's cheek, and winked at Frank. "Chins up. See you as soon as I can make it."

He went up the stairs, leaving the door open, and soon they heard the sound of hoof beats at a gallop fading into the distance.

"I think I'll go up and lie down for a while," said Ruth, smiling apologetically at her children.

"I don't blame you, Mother," said Helen. "I'll join you later. Right now, I think I'll keep Frank company for a while." Ruth went upstairs, and Helen leaned against one of the pillars which supported the floor joists of the house, as she studied the nude form of Consuelo, who was sitting on the mattress parked below her wall chains.

Frank was studying her, too. He was remembering the humiliation she'd put him through. Then he tensed as Helen picked up her skirt and held it at her waist, walking slowly over to the filthy Cuban whore. Frank was aghast as Helen pushed the girl over onto her back, then squatted over the brunette's head.

"Stick your tongue in this," she spat, her eyes daring the prisoner to refuse. Still she seemed surprised when the long, pink tongue snaked out and lapped greedily at her widely opened slit. It twirled expertly around Helen's fleshy little bud, making her tingle all over. Around and around it moved, then licked out and caressed daintily the swelling lips on either side of the slit.

Helen had intended to humiliate Consuelo, but now she was caught up in the pleasure of what was happening to her. Her breath panted as the expert tongue made passionate love to her excited flesh. She could feel the juices start to flow from her, and every once in a while the brunette's mouth would move up to cup her entire fleshy canyon and suck at it, draining it of its nectar.

Frank was fascinated by whatever it was that his sister was up to. He walked slowly over toward them, and squatted down to see it all.

Helen was too involved by now to think or care who saw what. She was breathing heavily, and the wind hissed through her teeth as the sensations built up inside her. Her eyes were closed, and a whimpering sound was issuing from her nose.

Frank's eyes dropped from his sister's face to her crotch. He stared at the beautifully enticing pinkness of her open slit, and watched as Consuelo's tongue lashed out and upward, sliding along a fleshy lip up to the top, then dipping in and caressing the tiny sentinel inside.

When her lips reached up and sucked at the fleshy splendour, he felt a thrill unlike any he'd experienced before. In spite of his recent activities, he felt himself getting an erection. He hadn't known that watching one female do this to another could affect a man so deeply.

Squatting down as he was, his slacks were stretched so tight that the erection was painful. He groaned, and Helen's eyes opened to look at him. Her gaze fell on his stiffening problem, and she made a tiny moaning sound, then reached out and unfastened his fly.

Her hand dipped inside, and came out with his hard lance. While Consuelo continued to pursue her involvement, Helen leaned over and let her weight go onto her knees, then she took Frank's wand in her lips and kissed it gently.

Oh, God! These people have really made perverts of us all! My sister is kissing my cock, and no one's even forcing her to. Oh-h-h! it's wrong, but it feels so good. Ah-h-h! She's licking it, now.

Helen had snaked out her tongue, and it began to keep time with the rhythm of Consuelo's caresses, which were stimulating the blonde's hot sex, causing her fluids to ooze steadily.

I can't help myself! My cunt is so wet and swollen now I don't know what to do, and that lovely hard thing made me so hungry I couldn't leave it alone. God! I hope Mother doesn't come down here, now!

Her hand was wrapped around the pale

shaft, moving the soft skin back and forth over the hard core, as she licked and sucked at the darkened head.

As the chained brunette worked faster and faster, she sneaked a hand over and dipped it into her own heated pool, where she fingered her hot depths while licking and sucking at the blonde's canyon.

Frank's hands had slipped into his sister's blouse and cupped the unfettered treasures there. The nipples were rolling between his fingers, and his excitement was at its peak. Then Helen's most intense moment came, and she trembled all over, just as Frank lost his load. It spurted hotly into her mouth, and she swallowed as it gushed over and over.

Then she rolled back on her hips, and sat on her feet and on Consuelo's chest, catching her breath. The brunette looked up at her and grinned, licking the juices from around her mouth with a weak tongue.

"That is a lovely cunt, with the so-soft blonde fur. I am very grateful that you let me eat you." She giggled, and let her arms fall out from her shoulders, the chains clanking on the hard floor.

Helen grabbed the arms near the elbows, then placed herself once more over the brunette's mouth. Consuelo began to struggle, and Frank wondered what his sister was up to. "What are you doing?" he asked.

"Something you can't do. I'll bet. I'm peeing in her filthy mouth!" Then she squealed as Consuelo bit her, and raised herself up away from the angry teeth, but Frank could see that a tiny stream still ran down the red canyon into the prisoner's face.

Then Helen backed away and jumped free of the angry hands which grabbed out at her. She stood at a safe distance and laughed.

"I think we'd better get her upstairs and cleaned up before the marines arrive," said Helen. Frank unlocked Consuelo's shackles and helped her to her feet.

"Come on! Wouldn't you like to get cleaned up?"

As she splashed in the big bathtub, he looked in often; and when she had finished, she came out an entirely different person. It was almost a shame to chain her up, again. Then she surprised him. She asked if she could wash her clothes before she went back down. He agreed, and she soon had them washed, rinsed and hanging on a line she'd hung up there in the bathroom.

When he locked her up, be told her that he'd bring the clothes to her when they were dry. As he reached the foot of the stairs, she called out to him, softly.

"Thank you. You made me realise how foolish and stubborn I've become. Bathing is something I should do more often!"

"If you took a bath every day, you'd be cleaner than you've been for a long time," Frank told her. "You've got a good start; why not keep it up?"

"I don't know how often they'll let me bathe in prison," she said.

He turned and walked up the stairs, not wanting to think about her problems. As he got to the doorway, he sensed that something was not right. He stepped through and turned to look both ways. In the hall between the kitchen and the living room, his mother stood. A man he'd never seen before stood behind her.

"I have a gun in her back," the man said. "Drop that pistol you're carrying in your waistband, or I shoot her!"

Slowly, Frank pulled out the Colt and let it fall to the floor.

"Your mother has answered enough questions for me to tell me what is going on. Call your sister up from the cellar." His eyes were strangely burning, and Frank wondered if this man was perhaps even more insane than Fernández.

He turned and called over his shoulder into the stairwell.

"Helen, you'd better come up here." His sister rushed up the stairs and burst into the kitchen. When she saw what was going on, her face paled.

"Get in here with your mother, *Señorita*." Helen obeyed. When she and Ruth were in the living room, the man spoke again.

"I'm going to take the young man downstairs. If both of you are not here, sitting quietly on the sofa-bed, when I come back up, I shall return down there and kill him. Do you understand?"

They nodded, and he guided Frank down the stairs and shackled him in the remaining chains.

"Juan!" yelped Fernández. "You have come just in time. Get me a doctor, so we can get out of here."

"To you I am always *Don* López Famosa, Fernández," snapped the distinguished man. "You have bungled this whole thing, and I will get you no doctor. You can lie there and die!" *Don* López Famosa looked at the other prisoners, and shook his head. He went back upstairs, and closed the door behind him.

Ruth and Helen were sitting on the sofa-bed, and fear was in their eyes as *Don* López Famosa approached them.

"I would advise you to give me no trouble, because I will kill either or both of you if I must, and then the young man. Take off your clothes and lie down on the bed. Hurry!"

Ruth and Helen looked at each other, then began to undress. They had thought themselves finished with disrobing for strangers. But they obeyed, and when they were on the bed, he took some cord from his pocket and tied Helen's hands to the frame at one end of the sofa, and Ruth's legs to the frame at the other end. Then he tied Ruth's right arm to Helen's right leg, and her left arm to the girl's left leg.

He removed all of his clothes, and placed the gun on the lamp table, pulling it close enough to be reached from the bed. When he turned toward them, they saw that he had the smallest piece of male equipment they had seen in this house. It was infantile!

He climbed up on the bed with them, and his face hovered over Helen's exposed blonde bush with its pink gaping slit. Then he lowered his tiny genitalia over Ruth's face, with his hairy, wrinkled sac lying on her chin.

He looked down at Helen's quivering flesh, and even from her awkward position she could see that he was pouting like a child.

"They've had all the fun, after I did all the planning, and they spoiled the whole thing. Now it's my turn to have fun!" The petulance in his voice was that of a maniac. They were now more afraid than at any time in the horrible days they'd just weathered.

"Now, Mama, kiss it for me as you used to do, while I have my little feast." He rubbed his pitiful equipment against Ruth's lips as he grabbed Helen's buttocks in his hands, and buried his face in her silky mound.

Ruth, frightened, began to kiss the wrinkled thing that dangled over her. It was so small and soft that she doubted if it would ever become anything useful. She wondered if his mother really had kissed it for him. What a way for a man to develop or rather, not to develop! She prayed that Charlie would come quickly. There was no telling what this madman might do.

The tiny thing slipped from her lips, and she could not recapture it with her hands tied. He half-turned and gave her a clout on the side of her face.

"You stop that! You just want to make me feel bad. But I won't let you! I'll kill you if you don't be nice to me!"

She stretched her neck out as far as she could, and finally managed to seize the miniature target, and hold it. She didn't dare let it slip away again! She vacuumed it into her mouth and held it tightly between tongue and teeth, then started to suckle it, her labours soon being rewarded by three or four little spurts of jissum, which she swallowed quickly.

Helen was ready to scream. This maniac had meant it when he said feast.

God! If he bites my pussy lips like that

much longer, I'll have to bust out and scream! Then the mouth lifted from her pained flesh, and he laid his head down with his cheek where his lips had been. He seemed to be going to sleep!

She listened for a while, and his breathing grew heavy. She decided to chance it.

"Mother!" she whispered. There was no answer, but the head on her pubis did not move. "Mother!" she increased her volume this time.

No answer. She wondered if he had struck her mother harder than it had appeared!

Then she heard it. It was muffled, and sounded far away. But it definitely was a sound, though it barely reached her.

"Hi-m-m?" was all Ruth could get out past her slippery little ward. And the dead weight of the madman's lower torso covering her face muffled the sound considerably. "Mother, I think he's asleep!" she said.

Ruth took a chance, and let her mouth open to try to converse.

"So? We can't get loose. That damned cord cuts into the flesh, and it's tough."

"Wait a minute,' Helen said. "I've got an idea." She told Ruth what they might do, and soon they decided to try it. It was a slim chance, and if he woke up, it might mean the end!

Chapter 12

Slowly, carefully, Helen inched her buttocks sideways on the sofa-bed, leaning slightly to hold the sleeping head on its pillow. Then she worked to get her leg close to the wall.

It seemed like an eternity, and it must have taken them at least a half-hour, but finally Helen's left foot almost touched the mirror on the wall. Ruth's left hand turned, twisting in its bonds, until she could place the back of her hand against the glass.

Then she pressed her diamond ring to the glass and tried to keep up the pressure as she described a triangle on the slick surface.

The crackling hiss of the hard stone on the glass sounded loud enough to wake the dead, but their baby slept on.

Then Ruth made a fist and pressed it to the centre of the triangle she'd cut. She pressed hard, but nothing happened.

Then she moved away a few inches, and told Helen she needed help.

"You'll have to swing my fist with your foot. Can you see where it has to hit?" she whispered. "Yes, I think so," Helen replied.

"God! Be sure! Darling, we may not have time for a second try if the sound wakes him up!

"I know. But I think I can see the exact spot. It's just that I don't know if I can hit it right on the first try."

"Listen, honey, do like a blacksmith does, you know? Swing right up to it the first time, but just touch it. If it's the right place, then hit it hard on the next swing. Like a golf ball on the tee, understand?"

"Sure."

Gingerly, the foot and hand moved out, then swung against the glass. It touched, but the hammer of flesh started to shake, and Helen rested her foot on the bed.

"I can't do it!" she said "If I swing it with enough force, I'll lose my balance on my hip, and his head will slide off, and that'll wake him up for sure!"

"Alright, honey. But can you relax your muscles and let me try to swing your foot with my hand? We've got to try something."

"I think so. Try it once."

Helen tried to let her leg become limp, and concentrated on the balance of her right hip, which held the crucial support for her dangerous burden.

Ruth lifted upward, and from the first moment that the dead weight of Helen's foot, ankle, calf, and thigh rested completely on

Ruth's wrist, she knew there would be no second swing. It was too much weight for the leverage she had. "First time or nothing, honey – pray!" she said.

She swung, and Helen's leg moved dangerously far, making the sleeping head tilt slightly. But as Ruth's balled fist struck the glass, there was a sharp crack.

The hand and foot rested on the bed, and Ruth tried to see if the piece had fallen out. No! It was still in place.

Then, as she looked at it, it dropped onto the bed! Both of them sighed and tried to catch their breaths. Then Ruth got the glass in her fingers and turned it around, arching it back toward her wrist.

At first she thought the piece was too small – that there wouldn't be enough reach. But she managed to get a shorter grip on the sharp glass, and then she had its edge against the cords.

In seconds, she had freed that hand and Helen's leg. Next problem was what to do first.

She could hold the glass against *Don López Famosa's* throat and make him stay still until Charlie came. But he might be crazy enough to try to out jump her, and she'd have to cut his throat. The thought was too much for her.

And when she visualized the *policía*

pouring into the house and seeing the scene on the sofa-bed, she had another reason to play the long shot.

Carefully, she turned toward her right, pivoting slowly onto her right shoulder, while raising her left hand with the glass triangle over and across the legs that lay on top of her. She had to get the glass over the right spot, or it would fall on the floor, or else somewhere out of reach of her captive right hand.

Just as she thought she was poised over exactly the right spot, *Don* López stirred, and the glass crashed onto the nearby lamp-table.

There was a loud noise, like a plank cracking in two, and then *Don* López Famosa was once more a dead weight on top of the two. There were heavy footsteps, moving swiftly away from them, and then the sound of the French windows opening and slamming.

"What happened?" asked Ruth, too frightened to move, although somehow she knew that *Don* López Famosa was not conscious.

"It was Osjami!" Helen said in a hushed voice. "He came in the hall doorway just as the glass fell. He hit our crazy friend on the back of the neck with his fist, just as his head was coming up. The way he fell back down, I think his neck's broken."

"Let's see if we can get out of here," said Ruth.

They managed to roll *Don* López off onto

the floor. Then Ruth cut another triangle of glass and popped it out onto the bed. She cut her ankles loose, then the other wrist. It didn't take long for her to free Helen.

"Get dressed, and hurry!" Ruth said. She was worrying about Frank, and wondered what might have happened if the prisoners had all escaped.

Helen was even more worried about her father. She hadn't told her mother that the black man had scooped up the gun from the lamp table. If he ran into anyone on his way out, he might have to shoot to kill. And Charles Hiram Longworthy could arrive at anytime.

Chapter 13

Ruth fished in *Don* López Famosa's pockets until she found the key for the shackles. By the time she'd located it, she was sure he was dead. She felt just a little sorry for him. Somewhere he'd been twisted, probably as a small boy with a less than capable mother. And he'd used his twisted mind to plot against the Longworthies.

If what he'd said had meant anything, this man must have been behind the whole thing.

She took the key and the Colt she spotted on the floor near the stairs where Osjami had missed seeing it in his haste. Frank was white faced and shaking when she got to him. He'd been worried sick about what might have happened to them upstairs.

He took the gun from her, and the key, and rushed back upstairs to look things over. As soon as she saw that Fernández was still there-holding his leg and moaning through whitened lips-and that Consuelo was sleeping peacefully on her mattress, Ruth went up to join her children.

She could hear Frank moving about in the living room, so she started to go to him. Then she halted at the bathroom doorway. Helen was just getting the bleeding stopped at the several places where *Don* López Famosa had bitten the lips of her sex.

"My God, honey! That maniac must have damned near bitten through you! Has it stopped bleeding? We'd better get you to a doctor right away. A bite can be dangerous."

"It's not as bad as it looks, Mother. It's several bites bleeding a little - not one bleeding a lot. Until I douched and started it bleeding again, I'd forgotten it. I know this towel looks like I'm mortally wounded, but get that deathbed look off your face. I guess his head lying on me there made it coagulate, and then the water got it going again. But it's stopped."

Frank appeared in the doorway, and both he and Helen blushed darkly before he excused himself and moved down the hall. Ruth shook her head sadly at the brief scene. These two wouldn't be comfortable around each other for a long while, if ever again. Neither would any of the family, probably. It had been a hell of a ghastly experience for them all.

When the *policía* coach rolled up out front Ruth panicked. "My God, kids! We forgot all about the pictures!

We've got to find them and burn them before anyone but your father gets in here! Frank, run out and tell him that. Helen, help me look."

"I think they're right over there in that drawer, Mother," the girl said. "Once I saw Consuelo putting some in there."

She raced over to the table in question and pulled out the single, large drawer so fast that the curling photos spilled onto the rug. They gathered them up, hastily and ran with them into the bathroom. They closed and locked the door, and started tearing them into little pieces. Frequently, they'd flush an accumulation down the lavatory.

Just as they watched the last ones disappear in a swirl of water, someone pounded on the bathroom door.

Ruth opened it, as she stepped out, Longworthy jumped inside and closed the door, yelling "Emergency!"

It was several minutes later that she recalled the fact that Helen still must have been in there.

Longworthy was unlimbering and aiming as he ran to the commode. It wasn't until the final relieving feeling that he realized his daughter was standing at the lavatory with her dress up, daubing at her tender parts with a bloody towel. Her eyes were wide with wonder at the sight of the once coveted member of her father, squirting like a fire hose in front of her eyes.

Their glances met, and both darkened and averted their gazes.

"I'm sorry, baby doll I didn't know you were in here, too." He'd started to get an erection, as he looked at his daughter's pinkly spread blossom, and it was difficult to shake off the last drops, now. He did it quickly, and swore as a last drop ran down his leg after he tucked himself away.

Helen had rushed to the door, and when she heard the sound of the flushing water, she bolted outside. Longworthy took a deep breath and followed her out. Ruth was standing there with a strange look on her face. "What's the matter with Helen, Charles?"

"I'm sorry, honey. I guess I shocked her. I didn't know she was in there until it was too late. She wasn't where I could see her when I went in. I'd been holding that back all the way into Cabañas and back here. Didn't take time for it at the *policía* station because I didn't want to leave you here any longer than necessary. I was about to spray my pants."

"This family is sure fouled up sex-wise," Ruth replied, looking at him as if trying to read something on his face.

"Some of this family got sex-wise under pretty foul conditions," Longworthy retorted. "I hope we can get readjusted pretty damned soon."

"I don't think it's going to be very easy or very quick," she told him. She didn't add that she was still trying to shake out of her own mind the way that Frank has stirred her with his amazing virility. Even Charlie hadn't stirred her up so, not for several months, at least.

She damned herself for a pervert and forced herself to take a walk in the weedy, ragged garden outside the living room. It was a good fifteen minutes before she felt the fresh air clear her mind. Then she watched several busy members of the *policía* leading Consuelo to one of their carriages. Shortly afterward, a stretcher was carried out to the other coach. Two police officers flanked Fernández as he started his bloody ride to the hospital – and eventually to the gallows.

Frank showed up in the frame of the open French windows. He ran to meet her as she came toward the house.

"I hope you got rid of the photos. I couldn't get to Pater to tell him in private, and then he went on inside. I showed the law where the dungeon was, and I guess that kept them off you for a while."

"We destroyed them all right. But don't mention it to your father. When he finally remembers those photos, I want to see the look on his face." Frank grinned and shook his head. "That might require a transfusion."

"The shock might just be what he needs," she said, mysteriously. And she wondered what kind of shock it would take to straighten her out. Frank, she observed, as he headed blithely back into the house on his own, seemed to be the least affected of any of them by the incestuous entanglements they'd been trapped into.

Suddenly, she almost felt all of her thirty-five years for the first time she could recall. Then she remembered that Charlie had promised to bring them clothes. At least she needn't look as old as she was ... if he'd also brought her overnight case. She headed down the hall searching for him.

Chapter 14

It was the end of the first of many weeks to be spent in Cuba. Weeks of waiting for the slow mills of Cuban justice to start grinding. Weeks that were to have been spent in Haiti, Jamaica, and other places.

Frank had gone out to see if he could make any sense of a Cuban play. Helen had decided to stay in and perhaps write some letters. Charlie and Ruth were dining with the Consul General.

It was only about seven-thirty when Frank returned to the suite, disgusted with the silliness of the play, and fed up with trying to follow the dialogue by the action. He ordered some sandwiches and beers sent up, suddenly craving a taste for the brew, and then peeled off his clothes and put on a robe.

He answered the door and took the tray from the bellhop, and set it on the table while he got out of his shoes. As he swapped the oxfords for a pair of slippers in his closet, he thought he heard something like crying.

She's probably having a bad dream, poor kid. No wonder, after what she's been through.

He opened the intercommunicating door to Helen's room, and started to enter and wake her from a nightmare.

There were no lights on in her room, but the moon was bright, and additional light poured in from reflections of the hotel marquee lighting. He took two steps into the room and halted.

Helen was lying on top of the covers. Her feet were drawn up snugly to her buttocks, her knees tightly together and raised. Her face wasn't visible behind the raised knees, but he could see that her hands were busy massaging her full breasts.

The hand nearest him was almost fully in view, and a darkly pink nipple was peeping from between her fingers. She was squeezing it and rolling her cupped hand on her breast, and all the while she was moaning low, but steadily.

"Oh-h... Oh-h... Oh-h... oh-oh..." on and on and on.

He tried to move to back out through the door way and close the door on her privacy. But he seemed rooted to the spot. And when her knees began to separate, he couldn't have moved, even at the point of a gun.

As the dimpled knees parted, the soft light etched the creamy inside pillars of her thighs, spreading as they separated, until they fell to either side, of their own weight.

The bright gold of the soft pubic fleece caught a gleam of light and sparkled. So did the diamonds-like drops of her passion that glistened at the edges of her swelling sex lips, and the lips were parting as they engorged with blood from her racing pulse.

Frank's pulse was racing, too. He'd let his robe fall open, and the silk sash lost its slippery hold further down. The whole front of his robe hung wide open, and the painful hardness of his instant erection was like a steel bar being drawn to the magnetic power of the sight before him.

He groaned as his feet moved forward, carrying him nearer to the awful temptation. Helen's face was visible, now. Her eyes were shut, and her constant moans continued as she massaged her breasts.

If there had been a framework at the foot of the bed, he might have been able to halt. But the way was open to him. He slowly moved forward onto the bed, pulling himself up to the gleaming wet pinkness of her spreading slit.

Then he caught the warm, musky scent of her, and he plunged his lips into the brimming pink vessel of flesh. Her juices flowed out around his lips, and he licked out his tongue and caressed her most sensitive spot.

Her moans were heavier and louder as he licked and sucked at her flowing juices, and then his hands were moving upward until he stole her breasts from her own hands, and began to knead them, and tweak the taut nipples.

Her legs wrapped around his back, and her heels pressed against the back of his neck, holding him snugly to the heated slit that was opening still further to his penetrating tongue. He knew that her eyes were open, now, as she replaced the moans with words.

"Oh, Frank! You're a darling lover! We shouldn't! We mustn't! But don't stop, for God's sake! Oh, it's good! It's so good! Oh-h! Eat me good, yes!"

His mind answered her as his lips and tongue and hands functioned like thinking creatures with lives of their own.

I know we shouldn't! We mustn't! I can't stop! Yes, it's good! Your sweet cunt is so juicy I can't stop eating it! Oh, Helen What will we do? We can't go on like this.

He felt the shuddering release begin. The tremors ran through her fine body until they filled her with tension. Then her hips rose and she pulled tighter with her heels against his neck, as she let herself explode into the clouds.

When her legs released him, he licked her warm, juicy flesh dry, then his mouth trailed upward through the blonde forest and over the heaving, panting belly. He tongued her navel, then moved up to suck heavily at her nipples

Oh, Frank, she thought. Your wonderfully hard cock is dragging up my legs! It's burning a trail up my thighs! Oh, how I want it! Damn me for a slut, but I want it! 1 have to have it!

Her hands seized his head and pulled it from her breasts, then brought it up to place his mouth on hers. As his body moved to make their lips meet, she felt his hard equipment catch in the hot groove of her crotch.

As their mouths tried to devour each other, she moved her hips until she got the swollen entrance of her passage touching the tip of the equally swollen club that lay in her warm, wet cleft.

"Helen! I can't help myself! I'm going inside you! Stop me!"

"No! I want you, Frank. I need you. Fuck me, Frank. Stuff me with your big cock!" She thrust at him to speed it up, and she took the whole length of him inside her with a deep, satisfied groan of fulfilment.

He sucked deeply at her mouth, then let his lips slide around to her ear. As he penetrated her, he spoke into her ear.

"Helen, when I get near that sweet pussy of yours, I can't resist it! I love the way it smells, the taste of it, the way it feels on my cock now, as I'm sliding into it. I can't leave you alone, Helen! What'll I do?"

"It's not just you, Frank. I get hungry for your juicy prick when I see it, even when I think about it! Let's talk about it when we're through. Please let's forget everything, for now, and just fuck together!"

He thrust into her with long strokes, relishing the soft, slippery folds that closed over him as he ploughed through. Then they were hurrying, rushing to completion, and he could feel her open up to him, deep in her hungry cavern, and he pushed hard to bury himself as he spurted out his seed.

When they stopped panting, he pulled himself out of her with a slushy, sucking sound and fell over on his side. She looked at the limp remains of his excitement, and the tiny blob of semen at its tip. A short string of the thick fluid trailed halfway along its soft shaft.

She got to her knees and moved down to it. Her tongue licked out and captured the soft flesh, pulling it into her mouth. She sucked at it until he groaned.

"Don't, Helen! You'll give me such a terrific stand that I'll never be able to get rid of it. Let's quit while we're ahead – or before we go any further astray."

"I was just kissing it goodbye, Frank. From now on, we'll just have to be extra careful. We mustn't go in each other's room unless we're positive it's safe. And we'll have

to avoid touching each other. But not too conspicuously, or the folks might catch on that something's happened between us."

"After having you, I don't think anyone else will arouse me so." he told her.

"That's what you might think, now. But when you get really hard-up like we were tonight, look around, and you'll find someone that will please you. I hate to think of anyone else having you. But we've got to be firm about breaking this off. You know that!"

"Sure. I'll be fine. At least I think I will. if I can convince myself of one thing."

"What's that, honey?" Helen asked, as she started to run her hand through his unruly hair in an old habitual sisterly habit. She jerked her hand away, and they grinned at each other.

"I'm good enough to get by, aren't I? I mean, y-you didn't want me just because I'm your brother ... like some sort of contagious perversion from what happened before?" He was watching her closely.

"You heard Mother talking to Papa back in our dear old dungeon. I'm a highly sexed gal who had a pretty strong father fixation. And you're a lot like Papa Longworthy. But you've probably got more endurance now than he has. Maybe it was partly that, and partly that you're just a natural born lover. Too damned good a lover!"

"I think I'll buy that. Your reasons, I mean. Because I think part of what draws me to you is that you're a lot like Mother. I don't think I had a strong mother image bit, but that episode with her did something that stirred me up good. It showed me one thing. Pater sure didn't get cheated on a good match for his sex drives, either."

"If we can all just force ourselves to toe the line until we can get readjusted, maybe we'll all learn from this. It was a horrible adventure while it lasted. But I'm not so sure the real torture isn't what comes now - until we can lick the tigers that were let loose on that farm." Frank got up and put on his robe and fastened it. Then he bent over and kissed the still juicy opening of her womanhood. "Goodbye, sweet pussy. Good night, sis."

"Good night, sweet brother Frank." The door closed on him, and she was alone. "Goodbye, lover," she whispered into the night.

Chapter 15

When the elder Longworthys returned to their suite, they both needed to shower again. Ever since their visit to the farmhouse, the whole family seemed to be unable to bathe enough. As she watched her husband towel himself Ruth wondered if the bathing obsession might not be a subconscious desire each of them had to wash away some other fixation.

She climbed into the shower he had vacated; it had taken her longer to undress as she tried to answer her own questions. Had she been able to break the morbid train of thoughts the last time they poured into her mind? Yes, but it hadn't been easy.

She'd gone in to wake Frank this morning, and found that he was in the shower. On the way out, she noticed the dampness on his sheets. As she leaned over and the magnetic semen scent rose to stir her, she bent down and started to lick the meagre remnants of the boy's dream.

She'd pulled herself away and walked unsteadily from the room. She'd beaten it. But it took several minutes of deep breathing exercises to get up the ambition to join the others at breakfast.

She climbed out of the shower and towelled herself dry, then put on the robe she'd brought in with her. Charlie had gone without his, but he would sleep naked, anyway, and probably was in bed right now.

But he wasn't there when she went in. She moved around the suite until she found him, standing just inside Helen's door, looking at the sleeping girl. Sleeping in the raw, like her father.

Longworthy stood a moment after she spotted him, then he silently closed the door and turned. He was startled to find Ruth so close.

"She's a pretty big girl to peep in on at bed check, isn't she?"

"Maybe so," he replied. "But something about her has been worrying me. I just can't put my finger on it."

"The thing about her that worries me you'd better not put your finger on!" Ruth answered. "Would you mind explaining that?"

"We were married before I was as old as she is, now. And she has yet to get interested in one boy enough to go steady. After the wild stirring her juices got, she's going to be frisky as hell until she starts getting laid regularly. I see enough of me in her to know that."

"That's it," Longworthy said. She's been fidgeting around a lot since we got back in the hotel. Can't sit still. And I remember now that I got the impression she was rubbing herself under the table at breakfast. Does it get that bad?"

"Not usually," Ruth laughed. "But I know what's causing that particular discomfort. She told him about the bites Helen had gotten from *Don* López Famosa, and explained that they were healing now, and very itchy.

"For crying' out loud! You never told me about that when it happened."

"I suppose there are a number of things that happened at that place which we haven't discussed in detail around the dinner table. Some of them might well be left alone. But I'll compare notes with you here in the privacy of our bedroom."

"Fine. For openers, what do you think about Osjami?"

"I think that I hope he doesn't get caught.

"That's not what I mean, Ruth. And you know it. Why did Helen stick up for him so strongly – before he saved you from *Don* López Famosa?"

"I think that she has the knack of sensing when people are basically right or wrong – good or bad."

"Too bad her clairvoyance didn't extend

to sensing the extra key Osjami had made in Havana and kept on him.

"That's your opinion. Helen and I both think that he had good reason to have that extra key made, and we're glad he did!"

"Why did he do it, then?"

"Because, if you believe the initial premise that he told the truth about Fernández's having something on him – and Helen and I do – it's a short step to believe that he could expect anything from Fernández, including locking up Osjami in those handcuffs. He just prepared himself for the possibility."

"Well, your judgment of him – or Helen's – might be proved by his stopping on his way to freedom to save you two. But how about his deserting his comrades in crime? Does that make him look such a fine fellow?"

"It surely does. If he'd been forced to go along with Fernández's operations, then finally decided to get away from Fernández once and for all, he wouldn't turn loose the very man whose sadistic tendencies he hated. And he'd stop on the way out to prevent a similar potential torturer"

"Very well. Really, I'm sort of playing devil's advocate about all that. I'm just as relieved the Negro is still free. But I wanted to be sure it wasn't just Helen's overzealous approach to his general welfare, or because she was hypnotized by his enormous cock, or something"

"What is it about you men that makes you uncomfortable when you think a woman likes sexy things? "You think a monstrous cock is so sexy?"

"No. *You* were the one to suspect Helen of being hooked on the black man's equipment. Remember? I'm trying to find out why such a fascination should bother you, if it were true."

"I'm not sure that it would. Look, why this 'Battle of the Sexes' approach? I think I'm pretty liberal single standard and all that."

"I'm going to see if you are. For a long time, you've made it clear that you like to eat my pussy. You've almost made poems about it. You're always telling me how the smell of my cunt excites you, and how you like the taste of it. Now, you didn't expect me to be upset about it, did you? Didn't you think that perhaps I should accept it as a compliment – a token of your overall feelings for me?"

"Naturally! So..."

"So, Mr. Single Standard, for years I've tried to get you to go off in my mouth, and I've succeeded only a few times. So, tell me why the objection. Especially since I happen to be crazy for your cock, and I love the smell of your semen and the taste of it in my mouth. So do you think less of me now that

I've admitted that, or will you accept it as a compliment?"

Longworthy was nonplussed. He looked at his wife with a crooked grin, and scratched his head.

"I know this is silly, but it takes some getting used to. I do see what you're driving at: The old bit about a man wanting a hot pants mistress or party girl, but a wife that's a virgin. Not exactly that, because you know I'm glad you love to screw.

"Maybe it's part of Mama-ism, something that's got us believing, subconsciously, all our lives, that you females the nice ones, the ones we marry, and our daughters, and all – are somehow better than men – belong on pedestals, and all that. And while we can love the cream that flows out of your gorgeous pussies, we are repelled by the semen we ejaculate, and don't want to 'contaminate' you with it. But you know, it is silly. If you like what comes out of me when you've excited me and made it come out, it should be exactly the same as the thrill I get from making you cream your panties and then enjoying the smell and taste of your hot little cunt, flowing all over for me. Dearest, I'm getting horny! Did you start this conversation, or did I?"

"I don't care who started it. Are you horny enough to let me steal your precious juice from you? I want to eat you, Charlie

Longworthy!"

"Jeez! What the hell are we waiting for? I've got a hardon that won't quit."

"I know. I've been watching it. I've been sitting here creaming my nightie over it. In another minute I'm liable to suck your balls right out through the end of that gorgeous thing!"

"Ha! I've got a picture of you killing the eggs that lay the golden goose!" He turned pale. "Oh my god! The pictures! we never got those damned photos they took of us. How in hell could I have forgotten about them?"

"Because you were worried about your family's physical and emotional condition. That's what drove the blackmail bit out of your mind. But we girls took care of it for you. They're all just little bitty pieces floating in the sewage somewhere."

"You're a doll. What would I do without you?"

"Like hell I'm a doll. I'm a real, live female, and the question is what are you going to do with me?"

"Well, what I had planned will be delayed a little. That photo thing scared away my boner."

"I think I can take care of that," said Ruth.

Chapter 16

Ruth Longworthy made a final dab with the brush in one dark corner of the canvas, then put down both brush and palette and stretched. She walked slowly around the perimeter of the glassed-in cupola that perched atop the huge house. Even the painting had failed to ease her restlessness, as it used to do.

For years, every time the tides of the moon had tugged at her, and the inescapable woman's nuisance rendered her useless for the complete kind of sexual romping her nature demanded, she had come up here and fought the irritability by painting. But when the first dark warning drops had appeared last night, right after a wildly satisfying sexual bout, she had not wanted to come up here.

For the first time in years, she felt a great reluctance to be isolated from her family, even by the small distance that would allow her to be heard if she yelled at them.

And for the first time since Frank's birth, she had not douched away the fluid that had been spurted into her, if one were to discount the instances that had occurred in that farmhouse.

She'd blocked her passage this time, she knew, as much to retain the precious semen inside her as long as possible, as to catch the red stains of her womanly curse.

What was happening to her these days? What was happening to all of the family?

They had all seemed to be throwing off the effects of their submergence into the depths of incest, even before they left Havana. Yet there had been a festering inside each of them, an imitating something that, like the oyster, each had coated to stop the irritation. But it wasn't pearls they had produced: just a hard, cold core of something foreign and frightening. And at unforeseeable moments, that cold hardness would become warm, then build such inner fires that it couldn't be ignored.

She'd watched all of them closely. They'd all watched each other. Not that any of them begrudged any other the smallest pleasure. But each seemed to have, at those moments when the coldness of that knot within turned to heat, a possessive hunger that made them reveal the naked desires they tried to suppress. It couldn't go on indefinitely like this. Either the evil forces within them must be exorcised, or something disastrous would happen.

All of them had come into this life with a healthy body and with a strongly sexual nature, which also should be healthy. Could those brief episodes of forced incest be the total cause of their breakdown? Would these incestuous hungers never have come to the surface but for the despicable Fernández?

Fernández! I hope he'll hang soon, or whatever it is that they'll do to him! If he hadn't done those things to us, we might be a happy family yet, today.

Shakespeare didn't cover it all when he said that 'the evil men do lives after them'. The evil that's done unto you lives on, too. It has a horrible life of its own!

She felt the stir of longing increase in her, and she tightened her vaginal muscles on the steadily swelling tampon within her.

I wish it were a cock-a big, pulsing, spurting cock, filling me up till I splashed over, till it flowed all over me! Oh-h-h! Will this obsession never let up?

Is it a weakness that we can never hope to overcome? And was it the same weakness that made us cooperate with Fernández? Would other people have endured the physical tortures even death – rather than perform the first incestuous act?

But it wasn't the threat of personal pain that swayed us – it was the threat to another. I couldn't let Frank be tortured to death –- so I gave in. I'm sure it was the same way with him. And with Charlie end Helen. We did it because of our love for each other.

But was it the purity of parental love and the love of children for their parents? Or the forbidden love of the damned working inside us even then, trying to break out into the open?

Could both Charlie and I have the madness of diseased ancestors in our genes, and passed them on, multiplied in strength, to those poor, lost children?

A scream seemed to be building up inside her, trying to burst out. But she felt that if she loosed it, she would let her sanity escape with it.

She bottled it up, and walked once more completely around the cupola, until she again faced the ocean. She watched the waves as they assaulted the seafront below.

Then she cleaned her brushes, covered her palette, and extinguished the light which she hadn't needed for at least an hour, since the bright dawn was beginning to illuminate the glass cupola.

She went down below, and moved through the halls, restlessly, wanting to go into every room, to shake the occupant from sleep and ask the questions she'd been asking herself.

She opened a door and slipped quietly into the room, then moved to stand beside Charlie Longworthy as he lay there, sleeping. His robust body was illuminated by the morning sunlight which came in through the open drapes at the French windows. His regular morning erection extended to his naked body, and she bent down to it, then placed a kiss on its purpling tip.

Just as quietly as she'd entered, she slipped out closing the door softly behind her.

Down the hallway she moved, halting beside another door. She hesitated, fighting with herself, then gave in and turned the knob. She opened it on its silent hinges, and closed it behind her.

Frank, unlike his father, wore a pyjama top to bed. But it did nothing to hide the virility of his maleness. His morning erection was almost the exact image of his father's, and she bent down and kissed it in the same tender but irresistible compulsion.

He stirred in his sleep, and she backed away a step, waiting until he quieted again before leaving.

Frank, my son, my lover. Your fluid is still inside me, in the depths of my hungry cunt. But it will soon be gone. The part of you that's in my greedy, evil blood, though, will still be there. When will I find peace? When will we all be free of this thing?

She left the room, and moved down the hallway again. Maybe a shower would help her. A cool shower.

As she started to pass Helen's room,

she saw that the door was slightly ajar, and looked inside.

A glass of water on the nightstand was half-consumed, and the little envelope beside it showed that a sleeping draught had been taken. Then a familiar scent filled her nostrils, and Ruth moved to the bedside.

Helen's nude form was spread-eagled in sleep, and the opened thighs disclosed the wetness of her pinkly swollen slit. A string of the white, sticky semen that had been spurted into her was trailed over one of the blonde curls at the edge of her canyon.

Ruth leaned over and inhaled the heady odour. Her tongue lashed out at the solitary telltale string, and gathered it up. Then she turned and went out of the room.

In the doorway, she paused before closing the door, and looked at the girl's sleeping form.

I can't tell whose it is. Either of them could have been in there with her. Either of my lovers That's the horrible part. Or is it? No. The real horror of it is that I'd feel the same way in either case.

She closed the door, and went slowly down the hall to the bathroom. A really cold shower might be best, after all.

The End

CUBAN-ENGLISH GLOSSARY

Bajar al pozo
To eat pussy
Buscar flete
To hunt for pussy
Comemierda
Eat shit!
Jodete y aprieta el culo!
Go fuck yourself!
Jugar a los dos bandos
To swing both ways (bisexual)
Te la voy a meter de mira quien viene
I'm gonna fuck you doggie style
Perra
(female) dog (bitch)
Perro
(male) dog
Puta
Bitch
Pinga
Fuck! (lit. dick) (Interjection)
Pingita
Small, tiny dick
Coño
Shit, fuck
Cojones
Shit, damnit, etc..
Vete a tu pinga
Go fuck yourself, fuck off
Resiñate
Very rude way to say fuck you

Calientapinga
Cockteaser
Malaoha
Someone who's really bad in bed
Malpalo
Someone who can't have sex
Chupar
To suck
Mamar
To suck
Singar
To fuck
Singa tu madre
Fuck your mother
Singao
Motherfucker
Singarte un caballo
Lit. means go fuck a horse!
Quimbar
To fuck
Me cago en nada
I shit on nothing
Maricon
Faggot, gay
Cabrón
Asshole
Tortillera
Dyke, lesbian
Cojones
Balls, can also mean "shit!"

Comepinga
Dick-sucker
Maricon singao
Fucking faggot
Mamalon
Dick Sucker (male)
Mamalona
Dick Sucker (female)
Pato
Duck (faggot)
Chocha
Pussy
Bollo
Pussy
Huevon
Heavy Balls (lazy)
Papayona
Heavy Pussy (lazy)
Come Pinga
Dick Eater
Pendejos
Pubic Hairs
Peste A Culo
Smelly Ass
Vete A Cagar
Go Take A Shit
Putona
Bitch, Slut, Whore

Just a few of our many titles for sale...

The Young Governess
The first title in our Past Venus Historical imprint. Kate Spencer's job as governess to a young girl in a large country house seemed idealic. However, she is soon drawn into the Followers – a mysterious group who take pleasure in forcing young women to perform perverse sexual rituals.
£7.50

Satan's Virgin Twins
20-year-old twins Pam and Daphne and their friends must risk their bodies, their sanity and their very souls by taking part in obscene blasphemies and horrific sexual rites in order to thwart the Devil's grand plan to reclaim his earthly dominion. Set in the 1950s.
£7.50

Orgy Girl
From the mansions of the Hamptons to the brownstones of Manhattan Karen Shaw is in demand as the Orgy Girl. In a spectacular, jet-setting round of outrageous sex parties and hedonistic fun with threesomes, foursomes and moresomes, Karen certainly proves herself to be no Barbara Cartland heroine.
£7.50

Salem's Daughters
The first title in our Past Venus Fantasy imprint. After centuries under the sod, warlock John Willard is more than ready to wreck vengeance on the decendants of the men and woman who sent him to the gallows, introducing them to incestuous perversions on a grand scale..
£7.50

Turkish Delight
After being cruelly raped by her callous husband on her honeymoon, Lucy Dean finds herself adrift in one of the most exciting and dangerous cities in the world: Istanbul. Drugged and abducted, she faces a life of sexual slavery, but first she must be taught the tricks of the trade.
£7.50